THE DAYDREAMING BOY

THE DAYDREAMING BOY

MICHELINE AHARONIAN MARCOM

RIVERHEAD BOOKS

A MEMBER OF PENGUIN GROUP (USA) INC.

NEW YORK ⌀ 2004

Fic
Marcom

This is a work of fiction. Names, characters, places, and
incidents are either the product of the author's imagination
or are used fictitiously, and any resemblance to actual persons,
living or dead, business establishments, events, or locales is
entirely coincidental.

RIVERHEAD BOOKS
a member of
Penguin Group (USA) Inc.
375 Hudson Street
New York, NY 10014

Library of Congress Cataloging-in-Publication Data

Marcom, Micheline Aharonian, date.
The daydreaming boy / Micheline Aharonian Marcom.
p.   cm.
ISBN 1-57322-264-X
1. Armenians—Lebanon—Beirut—Fiction.
2. Beirut (Lebanon)—Fiction.   I. Title.
PS3563.A63629D39   2004   2003055702
813'.6—dc22

Printed in the United States of America
1   3   5   7   9   10   8   6   4   2

This book is printed on acid-free paper. ∞

Book design by Marysarah Quinn

Merci-merci Hrag Varjabedian,
for your invaluable assistance.

4/9/04
ot 9°
23

MEMORES IGITUR MORTIS —
VAHE TCHEUBJIAN, 1946–1986

All of a sudden he discovered, not what he wanted to do but what he just had to do, had to do it whether he wanted to or not, because if he did not do it he knew that he could never live with himself for the rest of his life, never live with what all the men and women that had died to make him had left inside of him for him to pass on, with all the dead ones waiting and watching to see if he was going to do it right, fix things right so that he would be able to look in the face not only the old dead ones but all the living ones that would come after him when he would be one of the dead.

— WILLIAM FAULKNER,
ABSALOM, ABSALOM!

Who shall offend one of these little ones that believe in me, it were better for him that a millstone were hanged about his neck, and that he were drowned in the depth of the sea.

— MATTHEW 18 : 6

BOOK ❦ I

I

WE ARE NAKED like Adam and the blue wide band now becomes what it is, the long sea rises before us, the notfish become
what they too are, so that we see: water; white-capped waves
stretched out into infinity; but not salt, warm, sad. Clothes stripped
and bodies for the sun and sea and we run like the djinn, thousands of boys running to the Mediterranean, saying, we thirst,
we thirst and we drink the water and we laugh and gag, a gaggle
of orphans loaded onto the boxcars at Eregli and unloaded in the
Lebanon by the sea's edge. The water swallows us and we did not
see it before and we did not drink it before and though it was aw-
ful we will cry because with each gust of salt water swallowed it
becomes more and more what it is and not what it could be or
what it dreaming was or how after the push round the bend of the
mountain aboard that black hot metal beast and the flash through
the dark silent tunnel in the selfsame beast high in the mountains
it was: blue wide band, then the New Jerusalem, then sea of white
fish. They strip us of our clothes and they cover their mouths

with handkerchiefs (the smell) and wave their rods high in the air like some awesome pointed attenuated bat and we run, *yalla* they say, and we run and the millenary breeze like the millenary boys running, and the sea swallows us whole and the waves that are not fish tip us high and our testicles rise to the surface of the sad new sea beating for the progeny of the race. We are here, we say. Vostanig, I yell out to him: 'We are here'—the boys from the time before and we learn to swim and our bodies float in the salty air and the sun shines on this skin; we wait for the fleshy sores to heal in the briny warmth. 'Here,' we say, because it will be true and we will some of us have new Christian names and we will learn our trades and we will some of us regive ourselves of this now dead tongue and revived and here, we will say in the dead language: we are as Adams in the garden.

II

IT IS THE LATE AFTERNOON and hot today and summer,
1964. I am lying on the cracked tiles on the balcony and see my
neighbor's concrete barrier, his steel railing, hear the wife prepar-
ing the midday meal, yelling at the child to stop pulling to sit
down or I will smack you, the child having been smacked, crying,
the clacking of plates and cutlery and the sky beyond the railing
vast like the sea out of view. The tiles preserve some of that
morning's cool and I wish it were cool and that it were another
season; the heat penetrates the cotton skin and seeping into limbs,
heavy and unmoving, my hip bones nudge against my summer
trousers and when my sex strains against my trousers, together
they form some kind of unpious trinity. It is so hot to eat. There
is no wife to make the meal that I could not eat and the child is
crying again and asking for more in his prelingual shouts. She ig-
nores the crying child and beats the rug on the balcony and the
dust motes fall into my eyes and they are unblinking and my
limbs unmoving and she is telling him to hush, to shut it, smacks

the boy so that he is only louder. Were I to lift my arm I'd reach for the tobacco and brush the dust and soot from my eyebrows. If I've become as thin as a bedouin it is because of this heat. Because of my hand's inability to reach for the pack of cigarettes. The afternoons are spent on the tiles—the railing, the open sky, and although I cannot see her, the sea in the distance, sea and sky meeting in the summer's immutable haze.

I TOSS THE CIGARETTE BUTT off the balcony and my next cigarette is already lighted. I've got my right arm tucked beneath my head to pillow it and with the smoke entering my lungs and streaming out of my mouth and nostrils. I could alter the geometry of my bones, the angle of hips to knees, simply by bending the leg, and then I'm thinking of the girl who lived below stairs, the quiet beauty, the covetous green eyes, the left leg imperceptibly bent at the knee and longer than the right. I could love her on any one of the days ahead of me: her shy and prurient bosom, long thin and uneven gait, the flat and callused feet in the worn beige sandals; for those slim hips, down-turned gaze, the small and mostly hairless pubis: here on my back, the broken tiles pushing through and making relief on my naked back. The city quieter now but always there is a hum, a kind of unsettled bustling just out of view. The women the city over cooking their husbands' and sons' meal, slapping the child, the child quiet, the vegetable carters waylaid by a need for two tomatoes, the metal grates crashing down in front of the shop fronts, the automobiles hurrying home, prayer, accounts to balance, floors to be whitened later. All of this below my naked back, relieved by what it cannot see, the monstrous smoke in my eyes, not lifting the cigarette in and out of my mouth, loving the immutable haze I can make and thinking all the while of Yusef's domestic.

With the heat even lovemaking holds no interest today. Only my idea of the slim hips and tightened nipples and squeezing her ass. Not the body itself but the trace of it refracted and imaged by the retina and pushed into the mind and the mind making its own pictures then, like the moving pictures. My eyes are closed; Béatrice lifts her flowery skirt and she wears no undergarments; she is straddling my legs; her flower is opening for me; I begin to smell her and then she is moving up and down. She is so thin I can almost make out the convex impression of my sex beneath her skin as she moves, my hands wrap around each thigh, fingers pressing into flesh, meeting around her ass; she has pale white skin and when I remove my hands the blood rushes in red. In a few moments I am finished and my trousers are opened to reveal my hip bone and I hear the lady upstairs yelling at the boy again. There is a carter yelling out his wares. Tomatoes. It appears it is not so hot the milk will not flow and my wife continues our endless conversation, she is saying:

—Vahé, do you listen? (*and I am unable to*)

—Yes.

—Simply put: you are not right. You do not know how to love, or make love. I can't bear it anymore. Okay?

—Okay. (*notlistening*)

—You must go. Now. Tonight at the latest.

— . . .

—Do you listen? There's no going back this time. No reversal of fortunes. I can't bear it anymore.

—Yes. (*This is not me speaking*)

—Tonight. Tonight at the latest. Take your clothes and leave the key in the salon.

Another Vahé speaks, one speaks and one notlistens, the speaking one says:

—Juliana, it was not me.

—I'm so tired of this. I have gray hairs now. Wrinkles around my eyes. It could be your fault. The fault of a man who cannot love right. Didn't anyone ever teach you to do it right? All the boys learned at an early age, from some whore or another. Not the way you do it. Okay? My God. Where could you have learned? That stink-hole orphanage you lived in as a boy probably. You're still fucking crazy because of that, you know that don't you? My God. I'm not anymore. I can't, no more. No more—tonight, you pack tonight. You go. Sleep at the shop. My God. I must go to work—how did we come to this?

AND I HAVE WONDERED, how did I become this sort of man? debauched; the day after day of walks and walks; and the pubescent concubinal teat of the girl; a relentless specter; a monkey. And this question takes me to the boardwalk, the Corniche, and when the sea rises before me I am arrested by some thing I cannot think or name and on the nights I cannot sleep I find myself wandering along the shores and although it brings comfort it also surprises me with its terrible sameness, its constant in, this sadness; and I walk along the Corniche. I sit on the stone coping of the wall smoking until late. Only me, an occasional couple or group of young men. Drinking. Drunk. Drawn in by their singing and laughing, their intoxicated gaiety.

Over the years many boys and girls have disappeared into this sea. Vostanig. I hardly knew him or remember, Vostanig when he was a young man in he went; slip, the heavy filled skin. His mind. His heart and other organs. A boy who never learned to swim. Who threw himself of his own volition into the vast killer, the beautiful sad inscrutable Mediterranean. He was a bastard and I hardly knew him or remember. I never thought of his slipping away, I never considered his body or my own in the warm blue waters. I only loved the sea and to bathe in it, staying in the water all afternoon in the summertime. I would dive underwater beneath the waves and hold my breath and enjoy remaining there. Juliana searching for me sometimes from the shore. She is tanning, a white bikini you see more and more of now, we are more modern here each day and I am holding my breath; if I knew I could stay there forever I would perhaps consider it, to slip in. But I think the underwater would be temporary, deciduous time, and I want the sea only, in perpetuity, impossibly. And Juliana angry and frightened and because she doesn't swim, yelling at me not to do that why do I have to do that? And on Sunday afternoons we often go to the cinema. There are more and more cinemas now in the downtown near the Place des Martyrs and they have the American, Egyptian and French films and Juliana wears her new shoes and handbag and so we are more fashionable. During the dénouement I breathe slowly, hold my breath because there is a moment when I stop breath as if to make the celluloid surcease: my held breath to slow down the winding up——then a bolt of air, Juliana shushes me. I am sitting in the dark in the crowded theater and if it is summertime the fans are moving vigorously above our heads and it is stuffy and we sweat vigorously and I am not me, the man in my seat breathes heavily (Juliana shushes him, he notlistens) and that beautiful greeneyed girl in the swimming pool laughs and kicks and he pushes his mind into her laughs kicks toward me and she loves it, she is cool and it is bright. When the lights come on, I am brought back to the lingering taste of onion from lunch, my sweated-through shirt, Juliana says you always do that; why do you have to do that? And the speaking one says: 'I didn't. It wasn't me.'

There was no body to bury. I'm not really sure he did that: cast himself, slipped in. I never saw him after sixteen. I hardly knew him or remember. Perhaps he slit his throat; perhaps he lives here in Ras Beirut and holds a card for the yacht club; he is having mezzé at the Hôtel Saint Georges; summers in Aley; and when I last saw him he was shining shoes beneath a tin awning on Hamra, the scars still visible on his skull and forehead. The boy with the vile body. Years later I ran into one of the fellows from the Bird's Nest Orphanage and he told me, 'Did you hear the stinking lunatic killed himself?' I didn't recall Vostanig then, 'No,' I said, and walked on.

I dreamed of her last night. She was in the bath and naked and her hair was pulled back from her face. Her face was unseeable, the outlines blurred from the steam in the room. And she was sweating from the heat of the water between her breasts and her breasts were heavy and full and lay on her belly. And I was there, on her belly. Me as a babe, but not a babe: I was me as I am now, my chin hairs, sideburns, but in miniature, and I was lying on her belly, stretched out on top of her, breast to pubis, suckling. My hands holding her breasts, pulling the nipple into my mouth. My genitals against her pubis, my small penis small at her opening. My belly against hers. I was looking into her eyes and suckling and her milk was sweet and warm as the warm bathwater. My eyes rolled back in my head from the pleasure: her milk in my mouth, my milk on her pubic hair. It was the ecstasy that awakened me: the broken tiles; the southwesterlies die down; it is dark and still hot in the night.

I am thinking of this dream all the time. I am alone in the apartment, the beautiful young and naked mother is in the bathtub; I am on her body, small and enclosed, my sex tiny and her vagina a coarse pillow. I do not tell anyone about her and me there; I keep her close to me thinking, dreaming, because I cannot do it like some terrible jungle monkey anymore, because I'm not—and how did I become this sort of man?

III

WE COULD NEVER have been successful or disciplined in that place and of that place: discipulus: no learners among us, we could not follow the moral line. This is the orphan, small and not uplifted by the Sunday sermonizing directed toward our chastisement, our obeisance, toward Christian decency and good and the moral rod and listen to the mairigs even as they caned us, exhorted that we not fight among ourselves or steal or lie or cheat or gamble behind the bunkhouse or pleasure ourselves (behind the bunkhouse) and when that winter it was discovered that one of us was drinking wine from the flask in the rectory we all were beaten for his unconscionable sin.

(I myself having never understood Duty like a mistress and the zealot pays and pays to keep her; when some-starved and bruised and chanced hordes wanted and wanting only the smallest bit—always unpayable and requiring reimbursement reimbursing with this selfsame flesh: the orphan Body for the zealot's Duty. The same duty and psalm and speaking to us, exhorting with their turgid black rods and their notloves because not lovers of flesh and thereby inuring us to this our orphan's condition: the debt of our flesh and bone.)

Later that same winter, the boy Aram complained of a stomachache in the morning hours. He didn't rise from his pallet and we thought he was aiming for the infirmary and their extra soup ration and piece of bread, a nice mairig to cup your chin and us snickering and saying nothing in the cold morning, frigid water in the basins, we went to the classrooms single-file form. Aram still lying on his pallet come late afternoon and moaning, his hands on his belly, we now of one child mind believing in his suffering but the Mairig comes in and says get up boy. He doesn't rise up, lies curled in on himself and still moaning, although also now afraid we can see. She makes him stand, prods him with her walking stick and he stands up, bent over at the waist. Are you malfeasant, boy? she asks him. You tell falsehoods? He says it hurts, madam. Stand up straight. It hurts here, holding his side. She lifts his chin with her stick and asks him again of his falsehoods. Yes, madam, he replies and the Mairig quits the room. A younger mairig wipes his forehead with a damp cloth, hushing him with a soft voice. It is cold and we prepare for bed and huddle together beneath our blankets. The sea roars outside our dormitory windows. The waves rise with each hour and we can hear them crashing against the gray rocks and Aram making noise all night too. It hurts, he says. I hurt, Mama. Crying so much someone finally goes and gets a nice mairig in the middle of the night, risking a beating but running to her room, Aram crying on and on. The nice one comes in and seeing him runs out. They all came in then, even Hayrig, and he lifts the boy in his arms and carries him out of our dormitory. Later the following day Aram will die and I thought to myself then how I would never forget small Aram's body, and how I soon forgot it—the small body curled in on itself on the sleeping pallet, the sea so loud in the distance, the rocks gray, taking a winter beating. The Mairig is pale and quiet for a few days until a younger boy breaks a cup or plate and she lifts his chin with her rod and whacking him tells him that we will be reformed.

IV

WHEN I AWAKE I am alone. The whore departed during my
sleep. I notice she took my cigarettes and I get up from the bed,
the sheets tangled, the smell of her sex and mine is in the sheets.
I look for another pack and open and light one. Béatrice could
have been the girl I fucked. I thought of her while Rita and I
slapped it together. Rita is a whore like I am a bastard: she meets
me here at Émile's flat and I buy her European chocolates, she
says you are kind and taking off her shirt, her stomach heaves
over the band of her skirt, the fat on her thighs. Rita's husband is
a tramway operator and they come originally from a northern
mountain village. She knows her letters but just barely and she
doesn't resist the kind words, a flower I gave her for Mother's
Day, and then she is here, showing me her cunt, shy about it all
but also not shy in the least; I turn her onto her stomach and
shove a pillow beneath her hips, she says that I am a kind man and
that first time I wanted to fuck her from behind, but I didn't, not
then anyway. I chose her because of the green eyes. I tell her to

look me in the eye, she is shy, tries to look away. But if I am not getting her from behind I insist, look at me darling, and I am getting Béatrice. In the ass, in her mouth, sucking on her nether-lips. When I finally tire of Rita she comes to the shop unannounced. Pulls up her skirt when I am closing the door in her face, rubbing herself desperately. I know she needs me, needs this, in her sad life of cook, clean, serve her husband, wash the children, please the mother-in-law. But I tell her gently, even as I close the door, 'I am sick, dearest Rita, go away.' She is sickened by her own desire. The next time I see her she is wearing a religious ornament, I think she has discovered a more devout God. Today, however, she took my pack of cigarettes because her husband has no idea she likes the tobacco. We'd done it for a good hour and then she departed. She doesn't disgust me until it's finished and the sweating and the smell of lunch in our groins and underarms and on her hands; the smile of assent when we're done; in the moment after I've finished I hate her perfume, the fatty pubis, the dirty sheets—everything. I am glad that she must quickly dress and go retrieve her boys from school. I say nothing, turn away and sleep.

There is no end to my debauchery, so that I am sometimes disgusted with the body and its constancy. In my better moments I look at the sea and think that now I will do just as you did Vostanig. You were brave, not, as they claimed, a coward. Is there a more courageous man than the man who with his will unmakes his life? What else distinguishes us from the dark beast but our willingness, nay, our desire, to die for the cause and the idea: dulce et decorum est pro patria mori, eh Vosto? And you a man who could take the knife, put it to his throat and pull it across the skin, watch yourself unmake yourself: a bounteous act of will and desire. You your own sweet country. If I could be certain the waters would be endless in their grip then perhaps I would curtail all of this, this sex, this hard thoughts. Sometimes I am more lonely and I wonder where is the trajectory I followed? Why was I not left to rot somewhere on the road without signs, my bones invisible markers? Why preserve a child to become this sort of man? Debauched. Fucked. Where could I possibly find the stopgaps for this? I am not filled with rage, but ragged, unfurious, pathetic like you were. But you also were not sure and still you pulled that knife across your throat: the watery morphing blade. It is because I am a coward, Vosto. The worst kind of pathetic recreant— wanting to live because too afraid to not live. No patriot, this.

V

I begin my walk after taking my coffee as has become my custom. I walk down the Rue Makdissi past the French bakery and the tomato cucumber carrot sellers in the streets, the boys setting up their shoeshine stands, the basket vendor, the thyme and sesame breads in a heap on the wooden tray and the young vendors yelling out their freshness. I walk briskly; I light my black tobacco cigarettes and smoking, walking, watch the sun rise in the morning sky, glinting off of the sea, behind the buildings and later my back. The city is just beginning to rise, for now it is the baker, the shoeshine boys, the vegetable and basket sellers hauling their carts across town and me, a smallish man, a man whose middle has begun to soften and protrude, his long toes hidden in scuffed dress shoes. Soon I am warm and I unbutton my suit jacket; spring has begun to take hold and the tulips to emerge white yellow pink in Madame Renard's flower boxes; I take my right hand out of my pocket and light another cigarette. I make my way along the alleyway behind the all-girls French lycée and cross the empty lot with the withering grass wild thyme, the broken gate strewn glass bottles, the jacaranda is blooming. Soon I make the climb up Rue Sanayeh to the top of the small incline. There are no other people lingering outside the park, Ali the gardener sees me and smiles and ahlan-wa-sahlan it's warmer today, not so cold as yesterday and waves me in past the gate. There is the old and corroded sign above my head, reads *Jardin Zoologique de Beyrouth* and then also in Arabic below. Soon I have passed the closed ticket stall and the bronze of the French orientalist Jean Marnier who, according to the dedication below his likeness, donated the funds to open the first public ménagerie in the Levant in 1922. I walk past the aviary, the kennels where the sick animals are kept, the snake glass houses and the elephant corner. Each enclosure is tall and white concrete and white tile, the lone elephant in the jungle exhibit sits on her haunches waiting for the zoo to open and the crowds to assemble, she to begin the begging for pistachio nuts. I walk until I reach the primate cage and the small bench that has been placed in front of it. I sit and pull the packet of cigarettes out of my jacket pocket; pull out two Gauloises and put them in my mouth, light a match and inhale deeply. He smells the tobacco smoke or the sulfur from the match and soon Jumba approaches me. He makes his way from the hay he has been sleeping on to the bars nearest the bench, hauls his chain behind him. Jumba is alone in the primate cell; over time, Ali says, the others died of disease or contusion. But I know: the female one, a chimp named Urakayee, died last year after a bold attempt to push her skull through the bars of the cage. She did manage eventually to achieve her goal and perished from it—her head poking through the steel bars like a whore in a peep show.

Jumba has been in the zoologique since I was a boy and since last year I have been making my walk here on sabbath mornings. I sit on the bench, smoking two cigarettes; the sky is blue and clear this morning like the sea above our heads. Soon I see his hand extending through the bars as far as he can reach, my head is tilted to the sky. His brown skin is wrinkled and dry, his nails are dark and uneven. Without shifting my gaze I take one of the cigarettes from my mouth and extend it toward him; I imagine he notices my pale skin against his paw as he takes it from me.

I hear him move away from the bench. I look at him now. He sits quietly, his back to me, smoking. Like me he takes short puffs and looks around, looks at the sky above his head, a sky intersected by the lines of steel. There is an old tire hanging from one of the bars above his head. Cigarette butts litter his cage. It is generally known that Jumba the chimp is a smoker and so the adolescents come to the old zoo to offer him tobacco and take their photographs in front of the exhibit. He usually sits with his back to the small crowd, as he does today, which brings on the taunts and the poking with a stick. For a cigarette Jumba will endure the sticks and thrashes; he wears his scars with pride and a certain haughty superiority, as the rich ladies wear their armfuls of gold bangles at public gatherings. Every Sunday I pass the crowded churches, sometimes so early it is before they crowd up, as I go on my way up the hill and through the gate and I sit and I smoke and look at the sky. He smokes two or three also, as many as I will light for him. It is always me and Jumba, before the families arrive—the fathers with sons after mass is finished and lunch is eaten; the Jewish tailor and his brothers before it is too cold; the girls with ribboned plaits and a blue bow; the old village ladies older and smaller in their head-to-toe black, clutching the arms of their children and grandchildren. I don't speak to the monkey, our only contact is the brief touching of our hands as I reach out with the lighted tobacco. When I am next to his cage I take the smoke deep into my lungs, hold, and release. The silence on the sabbath morn is something to behold.

I have a forgotten picture of Jumba in my mind from when I was a boy and in the second year of the primary school, when one of the Sunday samaritans brought me to the zoologique with her two boys. The morning the samaritan arrived at the Bird's Nest all of us boys wore our hearts in our throat. To be chosen, to go out of the orphanage walls, to eat a hot meal, to smile and say yes and a piece of candy. We could bring back a toy, our lump of sugar and all of the other boys' envy for weeks as we retold the adventures we'd had. I had never been chosen on any of the days prior when the samaritans arrived, and I was never to be chosen afterward, but that day her boy, I can't recall his name, I see his clear skin, his skinny limbs (because he didn't want to eat his meat and yogurt) chose me, didn't like the boy the Mairig had wanted him to choose, he saw me in the yard, bent at the knee, making horses from torn paper and said give it here and I, my heart blocking my voice, handed it over and soon left with him and his brother and mother. I touched nothing that day. I had dreamed of that moment for so many years, I thought I would touch everything, eat everything, and yet I couldn't finish my portion at lunch. I left half of my bread on the table and later I vomited what little I had been able to ingest. I sat before the food on my plate, the meat and the green beans and pilaf and I wanted so desperately to be able to stuff it all in, preserve it for later, but hunger is never like that, you cannot stuff your cheeks for the following weeks' deprivations. I cannot remember the boy's name or even me as I was then—the shoeless, scrappy boy at the samaritan's kitchen table; what I recall like hard stone is the primate cell and the dark beasts as they clamored at the bars. I looked into their eyes and I saw a darkskinned boy, crass, yellowed in his eyes and teeth, dismantled, the sores and cuts and scabs. Jumba stared back and it was him, the older apes ignoring the boy amongst many boys, they wouldn't notice the shoes lent him from the samaritan, the sour smell of his angry lunch, how he sorely tried to keep it in, it coming up in the zoologique, he unable to eat the sweets offered afterward.

I didn't return to the zoologique for more than thirty-five years until last summer when Juliana said it would be amusing to accompany the neighbor's girls. It was not that I had refused to enter its gates again, I didn't return simply because there was no reason: a man without children or nieces and nephews does not go to the zoological gardens. My memory of the samaritan's children, selfish and clean, or the young chimp who looked at me and my borrowed boots that day two sizes too small, gnarling my toes under (Yes, they fit fine madame) was no longer a memory. Finally, on a Sunday afternoon we go and eat candy-nuts and marzipan and the neighbor's girls jump up and down like monkeys. It was Jumba I saw then, sitting near the bench, Urakayee quiet in the corner: their cage littered in discarded papers and feces and cigarette butts—all wet from the piss. I returned a month later on the sabbath, not remembering the monkey or the samaritan necessarily, going for no reason I could ascertain, just walks and walks and then I am there. And then again a month after that, and then the following week so that each sabbath now Juliana pressing me for my destination and me leaving earlier and earlier until finally Juliana doesn't do it anymore: and for no reason I can ascertain I am here, smoking, the monkey a short barred distance from my feet and you will still find me the ungrateful, unholy boy: the boy who never learned his lessons as he should have. The man who smokes too many Gauloises. I suppose that if I were a boy, different from the boy I was then, I would entertain fantasies about freeing the pitiful beast. Tearing down this citadel and running with him to another place. But I am not the boy who would close down the circus doors and beat the trainers with my whip, their white asses high in the air, me stuffing peanuts into their gaping mouths.

VI

THE SEASONS ARE CHANGING and it's cooler today. September is my preferred month of the year, the light is not too strong or the heat too hot. It is become the month of my birth, thus I determined it: 26 September 1917: 26 because I like 2 and 6, September for the not too strong or the heat too hot, and 1917 because it is a more than likely year—and so it is my birthday today. If today is the day of my birth then I will be forty-six years old and Juliana and I will go out to dinner tonight to celebrate with our friends. On my forty-sixth birthday I haven't yet begun my fascination with the servant girl, the monkey, or the specter; I am a working man in a shop and I earn an income. I get up and buy the newspaper from the kiosk, eat well, drink coffee and go out with friends, I have friends, I am not a sad and unorthodox man. For years I know nothing and I desire to know nothing about my childhood or anyone from that place, and I am a man who lives reasonably well. It is the epoch of living well, we are residents of the *Beyrouth où on vivait la bonne vie*—'La dolce vita, chérie.' I rent a flat in a modern six-story building, it is ample and light, we have furnished it and the sea can be seen from the west-facing balcony windows. The building is inhabited by three Armenian families, several Maronite Christian, two Greek Orthodox, and a Sunni Muslim: we fit nicely; we have nice things including a wooden coffee table, a sofa, two upholstered chairs, our woolen (machine-knotted) Persian rug, a wireless; we have many nice things.

When did the picture of Vosto first appear to me, as if from the ether? Because before this picture of him only blue sky or the dark sea illuminated by the halfmoon and nothing beyond what I could see: not ether and then him (Bedros Big Garo Aram Mairig Miss Taline and) created out of it and uninvited and not seen for decades and not dead, no, not vanished either—unexisted. Now I see him and often, but for those many years when I worked the long hours and later Juliana and our first apartment near the river until we moved here to Ras Beirut eight years ago and still the long hours: then I couldn't see him, I didn't remember him because, en fait, he did not exist. He and the others from that time and place placed in a walnut box (I made it) and never removed and so I forgot them completely; I unexisted them and they accordingly disappeared from the box and then the box itself disappeared. Was it on a birthday when he reappeared like some monstrous dark film specter? The film playing and replaying and forward and back and thus the unravel of now and Juliana and me: it was my forty-sixth birthday. We are dressing for dinner and Juliana laughs and complains about what transpired at the office and she is dressing in the bedroom, putting on a lovely new gown, her face is already painted for the evening out. She is ask-

ing me if I admire her gown (and hence her form) and I am saying yes darling and I don't expect you but you are here before
me—erect and holding your hands down by your side, fingers
pressed together tightly, as if you are waiting for someone; silent.
I am fascinated by your tight hands, straight digits that hardly
move. You're a little soldier boy and the other boys want to beat
your hands into submission, until they rise and cover your body
or spread out horizontal, like Christ on the Roman cross. The
older boys don't know I'm looking, of course to look would
mean my hands and face and Vostanig's pinkie has been broken
twice, his arm once and the mairigs complain that we play rough.
You sleep in the bed next to mine, I can see you next to me, you
are the only boy in the bunkhouse who sleeps alone. The rest of
us are huddled two by two: our best defense against the long cold
nights are each other's bellies, calves and string-bone arms. Your
lips are white and chapped all the time from the cold, the chilblains
are the most noticeable on your feet. The feet peel and redden.
The mairigs cannot force us to sleep with you, the boy assigned
to your bed bunks with Elias and Levon. You are a timid boy and
when you look at me one eye looks past me, as if there were
something behind that is of more interest. You are ugly, your
black hair grows in thin patches. Your mother is a whore, the
boys say to you, and Vostanig your crooked eyes are always filling with tears, you look up, perhaps looking for that whore-
mother who left you behind. The boy who cries is always the boy
they pull behind the back wall, the boy whose fingers are stiff,
whose pants are pulled to his knees day after day.

   He arrived with no satchel, only his torn pants and his red pus
sores all over his skinny legs, feet and arms. A boy who cries,

whose hair doesn't grow in evenly. When Vostanig first arrived at the Bird's Nest he was barely speaking. Perhaps he was five years old. He had been deposited by the front gate in the early morning hours. He said nothing for almost six months. The mairigs brought him in, they cleaned him up at first but later left him like the rest of us. We called him Kooskoos because he looked like a strange animal, his big nose and skinny body. He looks like a monkey, the boys say, and he does. Hair in patches, big crooked eyes, tears that rise up with the slightest insult. 'Whore! I fucked your mother.' Big Garo and Bedros in the bunkhouse next to ours have adopted him as their mascot, they drag him everywhere with them. The mairigs think it kind they have taken him under their care. They say to watch after him, he is your brother, although we have no brothers. Behind the bunkhouse he is their trained circus boy. They drop their pants and he, like a wind-up monkey boy, opens his mouth. One boy after another from the upper classes uses his mouth for amusement. He never tells me. I never followed them when I saw them call to him after lunch and disappear around the bunkhouse. He always follows quietly. Vostanig later at seven or eight. I see him kneeling before them. His mouth open wide. Cheep cheep. Do monkeys have big teeth? And he has trouble taking a shit. Here everyone knows everything, and if you can't take a dump the Mairig gives you castor oil and it smells all afternoon after it has its effect. He cries and cries when he shits on the pot. He tries to be quiet, but I can see his tears dripping down his shins onto his bare feet. I imagine the shits get stuck way up in his ass where it's horribly dark like a dark film.

Then I am in class and Mr Hovannes walks up and down the

rows of seated children. His whip is always available for the day-dreaming boy. I am the daydreaming boy but he can't see it. I look at him and nod. I am in the circus tent. A big elephant is up on his hind legs. I am sitting atop the elephant swinging a ball and chain. The elephant falls to the ground and I beat his flanks with my chain, the bull-hook snares his hide and up we go again. The crowd is laughing and cheering, the monkeys in the cages are singing at the top of their lungs. I can see Mr Hovannes in the audience and he is smiling and laughing and Big Garo holds his hand up to signal to me that he's arrived. We walk around the circle in the middle of the circus tent, the elephant's wounds leak blood. Raja, I scream at the stupid beast, hold it, hold it. One of the monkeys dies during the show, her leg ripped loose during the trapeze entertainment. The children in the audience cry and then laugh when Raja and I return on stage to lift their spirits. I swing the monkey leg above my head like a trophy, there are red-blood footprints that lead to the edge of the tent and Vahé, Mr Hovannes says, twenty-five plus thirty-nine and 'Vahé,' Juliana says, 'we'll arrive late. Hurry it up.' We leave the house within minutes; I hold the front door open for Juliana and she passes through the doorway. Vosto is with me all through dinner that night. I imagine him around every corner and seated at every table in the restaurant. There is the smallest unraveling during the celebration, an inappropriate comment to my friend the pharmacist, something about a street urchin and his wife. It must be my forty-sixth birthday, it is 1963 and the Egyptian singer Om Koulsoum performed that August in Ba'albeck. The famous diva sang for hours in front of the Roman temple to Jupiter and it was hot that night ('If I run from my heart, where would I go? Our sweet nights are everywhere'), Bacchus' temple to our left and Venus' behind—the wide and some vast broken colonnades. Juliana and I and the pharmacist and his wife had driven over the mountains together and wound down the Beirut-Damascus highway into the Beka'a Valley. It was the first time I had seen the legendary singer perform, and her voice that evening filled the temples and I admired the halfmoon and a month before my birthday, when each thing was as I expected, I was not discontented.

VII

Dear Mother,

Bonjour! I am now probably nine years old. I stand as tall as the apricot sapling in the yard. My eyes are light brown, my hair is also this color. I like to play football. I like to climb trees but the sapling is too weak to hold me. I know how to read and write my name, the city, the mountains. When I grow up I will be a horse trainer. The horses in the streets are sad and their whipping wounds are scabby.

Please tell me when you are coming.

Merci,

Vahé

(If you do not know me by this name, look for me by my birthmark: a small dark oval on my left arm, near the elbow.)

Dearest Mother,

Bonjour. Today we went to the sea and played in the warm waters. Here you can see the ocean floor through the clear water. The water is salty, do not drink it if you are thirsty. I can swim. I would like to have a pet, a dog followed me in the street the other day. Hayrig does not allow animals in the Nest. If I had a dog I would name him Roberto after the football player.

Merci,
Vahé

Hello,

It is unlikely you will be able to read this. You do not read, I think, or write. "A posted letter will reach its destination." <u>Find someone to read this note to you</u>. I am now probably nine years old. I have brown hair, the color of chestnuts. My eyes are in my head correctly. I have a birthmark you may recognize: left arm, small and oval, near the elbow. When I bend my arm the mark stretches and looks like a small balloon. I have small feet and hands.

Do not worry overmuch. Now there is enough to eat, I am growing. I did not die. If I could, I would play football every day and travel up the coast. Nothing is wrong with me.

Merci and arrive soon.

V. Tcheubjian (the family name—I took it from the store vendor who sells the best candies. I would like some candies when you arrive.)

VIII

VOSTANIG COMES BACK to me and re- and re- returns. I
know as he wrapped his delicate arms around himself at night,
I knew, what they did and his suffering and the boy who lived
there, that was me, who shared the same sleeping room did nothing because in that place the rule of bone, the law, was to survive
and only survive and we followed those rules, our bones, as our
fathers and mothers had followed the demoniac policemen, the
moving caravans—had walked out of their villages, and the
sound of the proclamations, the towncrier's call, this unheard because unthinkable, saying to them (and they saying it to themselves in their soon to be dead tongue): *All Armenians are obliged
to leave* and this new tenebrae to be sung later in the Lebanon
here at the Bird's Nest Sunday mass and so we also rule-followers,
bone baiters, even as we rebelled against every injunction in that
place. How many times, Vosto, did I take your bread? Double my
own meager portion and belt you when you cried? You would
suck on your shirttail, its tatters, and me eating your piece of

bread, smiling, funning, no room in my belly for remorse. We were terrible then, hungry. So many years of hungry and I forgot in the hunger, Vosto, any me that I could have been, I was made into the me I am still—Vahé Tcheubjian, and I have become him: the man who loves a sweetie, who fucks the boys and girls day after day and makes long walks along the Corniche at night; the man who makes cabinets, wooden boxes, paper horses; I can hear the waves hitting the gray rocks outside our window, Vosto. I'm not sure if you could love me now. Now when the food falls off my plate, but then for a piece of bread we kicked and screamed and you would look at us but you said nothing. You hardly spoke. I'd smack you sometimes only to hear you speak. Do you remember, Vosto? My speaking beatings? And you silent and you crying out that one winter when you were sick with the pneumonia and saying, 'Mama,' all night and I was surprised by your voice, its dull and deep pitch, bigger than your small scabby body. 'They're coming again,' you screamed in the dark. The other boys laughing, taunting you as I whipped you at mealtimes. You sucking on your shirttails, leaning against the red brick mess house.

So today Jumba died (17 mai 1964). Today is sabbath and on my walk up the hill I stopped, and I never stop as I make my way up the hill, Rue Sadat, Rue Danant, but an ache in my hip, that darting pain which stops the leg, and then the body and mind catch up and sit down, go into the café for a fast coffee, seated in the corner. I was an hour later than usual and Jumba seated in his corner, chin resting on his chest, hands interlaced on his belly, asleep. I sat on the bench and smoked one, then two, then three and finally four and you came to me Vosto, you returned as you had repeatedly returned since September of last year. Because another boy, a smaller boy, made off with your bread this time, not me but a short boy, daring and younger than you, and we both knew that only I had the right to such an act, you said, 'Master he's taken your share.' I was standing by myself for a moment and you approached, kneeling at my feet. You looked up at me, your dark brown eyes, your patchy hair, your tears as always and I let you for a moment look into my eyes, or I looked into yours and saw you, Vostanig. Pathetic boy. Half-starved, scabbed raw. Hungry, hungry—in your eyes and belly. Vosto, what would you have done for a mother's teat? What we all would have done in that place: cut off your finger and handed it over as blood payment: here, take this from me. You saw your mother jump into the Euphrates River, she instructed you to jump also and you didn't, wretched boy. You are standing on the banks of that body-filling river in Anatolia. Thousands of women bodies float by you: some bloated and blackened, some young and shy screaming girls. You stand on the banks and your mother is gone within seconds. And you never get her back, not for all of your crying or sucking on shirttails—when Jumba died, I felt again my hatred for you. Jumba could have been forty or forty-five years old. Perhaps we were the same age. I wanted to bury my cigarette in his already rotting flesh, in his cradling hands and small paunch belly.

You were stupid Vosto, on that day and on many others, and when the boy Arshag finally came after you with his stone, your constant whining about the black bread his final undoing, when he came at those eyes of yours poking out of your head as if they'd been blown up with air like some bloated sea carcass, he thought you would flinch or turn away and unflinching he took the sight from your left eye. Then I hated you most. Standing at the bank of the river, your mother's body careening away. You there saved by a Turkish peasant; you here, half dead, half eaten, blinded. Vostanig: you were everything we hated. There will be no burial for Jumba, Ali tells me. They'll burn him with the garbage. 'Did you know,' he says, 'he was a babe when they captured him? Still sucking on his mama's teat.' A few years later they brought an older female from the same place and 'I swear to you,' Ali says, 'I saw the chimpy smile when the new one was let in the cage. She didn't last long. How he carried on when that one died, we had to put him in the lock room for a week and he made a lot of noise still. Then he became like you knew him, sullen, and he'd bite your hand for less than a pistache.'

IX

I DREAMED LAST NIGHT that I was chained by the ankle to the bars of my cage. I could not stand or lie on my side. I was in the cage for thousands of years in my dream, interrupted by my guards and their garbage meals for me: desiccated pita crusts, cheese, tinned vegetables and the occasional lamb hock. I was blindfolded and unable to move, I could never see my captors' faces, only their hands as they threw my meals onto the floor and beat me. They gave me four cigarettes a day and I smoked them slowly, savored the in of the smoke, there were no spectators and I was not in the zoological gardens. When they left me to myself I could lift the blindfold and observe my brown paws, the finger-nails were cracked from the years in the place and the garbage food and I noticed I was fat and becoming fatter and fatter, I never moved, I couldn't stand or lie down, only sit and stare and if I managed to replace my blindfold before the guards entered I was beaten less frequently. My dream was interminable, it was a millenary dream for the millenary boy and here was no sun or light, without the sea or waves and no untutored servant girl (and I could love her: Béatrice); no humming bird in my memory to save it from its desertion and then anguish. I could not read; I was an unschooled animal. Only sentient and sitting in the puddles of urine and my feces: my filth disgraceful and unable to say so or speak anything or cry out—I missed you most in this dream, my animal dream, there was no one to free me or see me, no one noticed, and isn't pain always unseeable? *I do not know fear because I do not not know it* and I was maddened by it ultimately. And when I awoke I awoke maddened and knew it was in me. I was on my bed and had sweated through the sheet to the mattress. The chains were still in me and I would still eat garbage for lunch, I was, en fait, Jumba, he was dead and become me—speakable now, my hands his paws, the telephone ringing and Juliana's 'Allô?' and I was as afraid as I had ever been because I knew it now. The sleeping man awakes to the animal and he begins to recollect the distant parts of himself: the orphan fledgling indolent ape; I had hidden it away in a box for so long, and it recovered by a millenary dream, the 26 September, the dead animal in his cage, invisible memory stones pulled forth one by one. *The war begins its wage in me, the boy made from war and returning to the contest of his birth.*

א

UNBEKNOWNST TO ME. I am sick and it is unbeknownst to me. What can I see? Your face Juliana in the evening light is clearer and unwrinkled, you are younger. After wine and arak, your face is blurred before me and my loins tighten: you are desirable and we fuck it. After work we are tired and irritable and you seem to me uninteresting, heavy, the way you are twisting your hair. At Uncle Sam's Restaurant across from the American University: you are lifting a soft drink to your lips and I see you for the first time, I am lifting a drink to my lips, I am standing by the door, everyone is loud and some people are speaking in loud hard English and some people cursing loud in Arabic and there is a French song playing on the radio; you are beautiful; it is Salvatore Adamo and his recorded voice is singing. I see beauty, the pulled-back hair and it is teased high, your cheekbones unrouged for me, your lips and your small square teeth: I see a trim woman. And when you walked into the kitchen and I was fucking Béatrice fourteen years after that? I saw you, but who did I see walking into our flat? The girl from Uncle Sam's? The officious secretary arrived home early from work, she is tired and she looks tired? The obedient wife who's gone to buy me a gâteau? My sad darling. And then I was pleasured, you saw me take my pleasure. I am hopeful that you also could see me then: my taut and older flanks slapping against the girl's backside. I am glad you saw me there, that was also me Juliana, and it is with great and hungering shame. You said nothing. You walked out and closed the door and we didn't speak of it. We never did. But since that time it has been with us: our silent banshee. She wails outside the balcony windows. At dinner that night I talked about Mr Gembali's boys and the new shop and I talked on and you listened. I said Justin has long been Gembali's favorite. I said the boss complained of how his hands ached from the meting out of so many punishments to his favored son.

Juliana: you have tried to be the good woman, the good Eve, from the beginning. In the beginning, my darling, we made the bordello and in the Beirut not so far from that beginning they still turn a fine business. Here in Beirut business is good!

WHEN SHE WAS ten years old she still used the step stool at the sink. Do you recall? On Sundays she would come to help you sometimes and she brought her stool along. You loved and admired all of the children in the building, you brought them special treats on the holidays and took them shopping or to the cinema when their mothers prepared for a special event, yet it never occurred to you (or to me) that this servant with the step stool was childish. At least we never spoke of it, and the girl hardly spoke at all. She was a quiet bird, even now she is a quiet bird. That she spent all of her days in the small kitchen downstairs in the small flat of only two dormitories and one lavatory, a salon; that in the evening she pulled her bedding down from the cabinet and slept on the kitchen floor; that the working and working: clean the flat, ironing, pounding the kibbé, washing up and washing the clothes was rarely interrupted, for years. She was a trained girl and a quiet bird: up before dawn, the last to sleep at night. How many times was she allowed to go outside the flat in those years? Perhaps once in a month? On her days off which she could not take because where is a ten-year-old girl without family going to go, what will she do, alone in this city? 'No, better she is with you on the second Sundays,' Madame Yusef tells you. 'After mass we often go to my mother-in-law's for lunch, and that girl loves the kitchen.' So she never left the flat downstairs except to come upstairs and for a few Lebanese lira, pound our kibbé and wash up, tugging her step stool along. Yet you did recognize something childlike: you gave her chocolates. To be so powerful as to engender love through a piece of chocolate—you were the kindest patroness, and didn't you give her a scarf once? One of your shawls another year? Weren't we generous then, darling?

I would like to know the notknowable; these are simple, primary inquiries: where are the gods? And without them: where are we? If only heaven and the houris, if only to see them, in a place—a mama a baba and—they could all await me in a queue like the queue outside the cinema, next in line to the houris? Each one beholden to me by his blood, each one in love with me because of it. I endeavored to believe in Him, I prayed and attended the mass and I listened to the priest during the marriage cere-

mony; I endeavored to be good and obey but I could not recon-
cile; I cannot be reconciled; and I have endeavored during the
years of cabinetry making, each piece distinct and beautiful, every
shave of woodcut like a caress, every caress a work of these hands
and the rich are made proud in displaying their hardwood beau-
ties and handwoven woolen rugs at all of their soirées. (Do they
think of the knotter? The young girl with her small fingers makes
the colored knots, she is bent at the waist. Do they think of the
cutter?) Béatrice: I didn't think of you in that kitchen, did not
give your life in that place a moment of my thinking. I could see
you but I couldn't see you (*the knotter, the cutter*).

I am an open heart and unassailable, I imagine that I cannot be
assailed and it is a lie: the small pitiful and open-heart boy is still
me. I am no different from the boy the Mairig beat more than
once: bruised and stupid and beaten-up. It is hot today. I am here,
alone, lying on my back on the balcony and smoking a cigarette.
It is a usual day down below and I hear all of the usual sounds of
lifted-up grates and children and the car horns blare and the buses
one street over and the cucumber tomato carrot sellers: the hours
pass without my notice or participation: there is something terrible in the relentless hours, like a mask or unflying unfeathered bird.

Juliana, finally this: the banshee that is between us? It is my
death she portends. Her wails for me only.

XI

THERE IS NO DESIRE today or yesterday. Days without desire and no matter the amount of manipulate and draw upon and stimulus: I cannot create the force to pull me into the world. I am afraid, here in this white-tiled box room. I have never thought so much about color as I do now in this world devoid of color—of the coarse crenulated orange rind; of brown nut hulls piled into the crystal ashtray; of the red-bead pomegranate seeds. My mind spins off and off and takes me deeper into myself, down into cells. I am the sentient mammal in the white-tiled mind room. It is tight and now dark, no white or light, then pulses tightens, my head and shoulders pain me; I am afraid and sad, no water to hold me. The pulse and tighten, my head and shoulders pain me. I cannot see, I could never see yet so that does not frighten, and the hold so tight against me is tighter and then tighter than before and before this eternity evens out it is all of the air sucked in, I am sucking in air and it is open, open and fear of this wideness and out. It is horrible, hour after hour before the hours —then the wide open and gravity heaves the body and outside because an inside: the beginning of difference, of the double world: out and in, what I see and what I feel, you and I. Wideness and wildness. Whiteness again and I am in the white-tiled box room. It is the bathroom. I am relieving myself, holding myself and relieved. Now zipping my trousers and I am pulled up into the surface of things: the porcelain toilet, the bathtub to my right, the sink is dirty. I look into the mirror and see the gray eyes and the nose pulling this way, the brown spot on my upper lip and between my brows from the sunning and years of seaside. I look in the mirror and do not see into me out of my mind, more in the mind than I have ever been. It was me as I was then: a babe on his uterine journey from the sea to the shore. Because: there was a moment when you were mine and I was yours, for at least those uterine months we were together, I could say we were of one flesh. How pathetic is the man who seeks love. I am the man seeking love. In the toilet I remember, it is prelingual because it is impossible— the babe leaving his mother's womb, pushing through her vagina, her vagina holding me tightly, kissing him fiercely goodbye. The goodbye. Did you ever suckle me, Mother? Some woman suckled me, I hope fiercely that it was you.

XII

I AM SITTING ON MY BED AND

I am sitting on my bed and shirtless it is hot and we are smoking
as usual. The smoke has filled up our bedroom so I can just make
out her face through it and her fingernails are painted, she is rubbing her hands up and down her thighs and her thighs are slim
and fine and rubs the skin and she takes her red fingernails and
hangs them in front of me because they shine in the smoky room
and I am aroused because she is not wearing panties or a brassiere
and her breasts are large and reach down and touch one and lift it
to my mouth for suckling. She suckles me but instead of milk it is
water coming down from her teats and I tell her to give me the
milk because I want that more and she says she cannot and rubs
my head and she is singing to me—a lullaby from the dead language but she is singing it in Arabic and then because I want the
milk and not the water I bite deeply into her chest and she sings
to me and I am sucking the blood now through her open wounds.
Singing new spring arrives beautiful spring, isn't it? It is what I

desire more than anything. I drink her blood until she is empty and dead. But she awakens after dying and tells me that she loves me. That she has always loved me and she doesn't leave, she never leaves our bedroom. We are always in the bedroom and my mama loves me here and every night she comes and although I don't like to kill her I do because she has the blood and I am thirsty and also hungry. In the Lebanon blood never changes to water but here I can have it because I am good. Here I am good and she loves me here. She never leaves our bedroom. We are always in the bedroom and my mama loves me here and every night she comes and although I don't like to kill her I do. Because she has the blood and I am thirsty and also hungry; in the Lebanon blood never changes to water but here I can have it because I am good here. I am good and she loves me here I am sitting on my bed and she never leaves our bedroom we are always in the bedroom and my mama loves me here and every night she comes and although I don't like to kill her I do because she has the blood and I am thirsty and also hungry in the Lebanon blood never changes to water but here I can have it because I am good here I am good and she loves me here I am sitting on my bed and she never leaves our bedroom we are always in the bedroom and my mama loves me here and every night she comes and although I don't like to kill her I do because she has the blood and I am thirsty and also hungry in the Lebanon blood never changes to water but here I can have it because I am good here I am good and she loves me here I am sitting on my bed and she never leaves our bedroom we are always in the bedroom and my mama loves me here and every night she comes and although I don't like to kill her I do because she has the blood and I am thirsty and also hungry in the Lebanon blood never changes to water but here I can have it because I am good here I am good and she loves me here I am sitting on my bed

XIII

The speaking one said:

—No, not terrible, because I am one of the lucky ones. I learned my trade and I'm healthy as a horse.

—Yes, you seem it (smiles and raises her right hand, her nails are painted dark red and shiny). How old were you when you left?

—Sixteen.

—Where did you go?

—I shared a room in the back of Mr Gembali's shop, in those days it was a small operation. Just me and another boy, Émile, and Mr Gembali.

—Who cooked for you?

—We did mostly and when Madame Gembali took pity on us we ate with them on Sundays. Her cook was fantastic, I would eat enough for ten on Sundays!

—You do seem healthy (touches his cheek with her right hand, the nails are glossy and soft against his skin). And now?

—Now I bring someone to the flat and she does everything

(smiles), would you like another cola? (looks down at her legs, the slip rises above her knees, her legs are crossed.)

—Yes, please.

—Pardon me.

— . . .

—Vahé: you think about them?

—Here, please: no.

—Thank you.

(she is biting her lip, her lips are red and shiny and match her nail polish. She takes a sip of the cola drink.)

—Would you like another?

—Vahé—no thank you—when is your birthday?

—26 September.

—Soon, in one month's time! Mine is May (she takes another sip of her drink and looks down at the tabletop). I love this chanson, *'Tombe la neige, tout est blanc de désespoir.'*

—(smiles)

—It's my favorite by Adamo.

—You are lovely, Juliana.

(she looks down, he takes her right hand into his hands.)

—Beautiful. Are you hungry?

—No, merci. No one to tell you what to do then? You are without obligations?

—I can do as I please. (smiles)

—I had to fight to study at the secretarial school. My mother didn't like it one bit but my uncle convinced her that these days women are working and we need training. We are becoming more modern here, he told my mother, the Lebanon is independent these last four years and times will change.

—To the cinema then?

—Is it time already? Have you seen his others? I saw *Notorious* when it came here last year and it was magnificent.

—Shall we go? (takes her hand. He feels the smooth nails against the pads of his fingers. He likes it. She is lovely.) *Yalla.*

—Did you think it was fine? I have loved every film with Cary Grant in it. Were you surprised by the outcome? I thought it sad beautiful.

—No, not at all, this way. Yes, chérie.

—Right here, down Hamra. (they are not holding hands. It is hot in the streets.) It is so hot still, even at night. I'll be so happy for the cooler days of September, and your birthday also! We shall celebrate wildly, I love the wild parties!

Thinks: *it's untrue because: they met in 1949 in Ashrafiyeh behind the Azadamard Club where Juliana lived with her mother younger brother and five other Armenian families in that flat and the Second World War only four years gone and there was no cola factory then and the girls didn't paint their fingernails then and the first wave of refugees from Galilee and Jaffa filled the streets and begging in the streets lived in the white tents on the edge of town and they would have taken a service in any case to the cinema and the Hitchcock film came out in '51 and he never once was invited to the home of Mr Gembali for dinner and he never brought a servant to his flat and an Armenian girl would not have thought it terrible because she would know—(the events of summer 1915, Ottoman Turkey: the Catastrophe—the Armenian clans decimated; deported; marched through the Der-el-Zor desert; thousands of children left behind in orphanages until the orphans themselves were deported in 1922; until no Armen-ian remained in that place; their two-thousand-year presence erased from the land like one erases pencil drawings from coarse paper)— like she knows her name and Juliana born here in 1927 and given her not-Armenian name because of the American nurse at the American University of Beirut Hospital and she knew it also, with her accented Arabic and the taunts as a small girl: that we all of us were out of place here, orphaned in one way or another and*

XIV

'I'M SORRY that I made you cry.'

I saw you today in front of our building. You left the flat of your own volition, didn't you? Or is it that Madame Yusef is now too lazy to go out and sent you on an errand? And I saw how you were dawdling, not wanting to step inside the lobby. I followed you for a while. You were looking into the boutiques and turning your head away if a seller approached the vitrine. For a while you were in front of the women's hair salon, the new one on the corner with its fancy sinks and mirrors and the middle-aged ladies getting their hair coifed during their weekly appointments; the photographs of the Egyptian movie stars enlarged and smiling from the three walls. You were staring through the glass, at the fancy hair-styling chairs and the mirrors and the neighborhood ladies were laughing, weren't they?, while their hair was washed and dried and colored and adorned. They were smoking cigarettes and so you peered through glass and smoke to see them and the movie stars reflected. The boy brought the tray of coffee every so often. Your hair was plaited as usual, long down your back, you had long ago given up your headscarf in a city where no one, not even the most devout, wears them anymore. Now your head is bare and your calves are also bared and beautiful, taut and slim, the muscles stretch along your leg and widen slightly toward the knee, taper down and disappear in skin and bone and beneath your socks. I could not help but follow the path of your calves, the soft of your knees, the bend of your yellow dress toward the apex of your thighs, your thighs barely meeting, a kiss of flesh, and then your sex, small and enclosed. This was the path I made.

I didn't mean to hurt you, I'm sorry that I made you cry: can you hear me singing it? I'm behind you singing it, this song everyone has playing on their radios these days: 'Je n'allais pas te faire mal, peut-être ne m'aimes-tu pas non plus.' You dragged your feet home, the closer you came to the portal the slower your gait, your uneven gait with the slight heavy push by your left and longer leg. Your calves tense and resist the pull up and push down on the pavement. But where else to go? Did the boy on the corner give you a smile as he often does? The grocer's son? I've seen him, he delivers your groceries and ours, I've seen him grow up. He used to play in front of his father's shop with a crude wooden train and now he hauls the crates of fruits and vegetables and dry goods for a small tip. He's not for you, my dear. A grocer's boy? Keep walking. Don't stop or look at him. I see you keep walking, he looks up from rearranging the lemons and eggplants. You draw yourself upright, you don't look at him but I can see it is deliberate, done to draw his attention. You lean away from his stall as you walk by and he consequently leans into you and whispers something, I can't hear it, I'm up on the balcony and staring down, I'm a block behind you hiding in the doorway of the watchmaker's, I'm sorry that I made you cry I'm a jealous guy, can you hear the song from my salon? I'm tempted to throw the potted azalea but it is unlikely I'll make my target from the four stories up. You continue, but are you smiling now? The radio is blaring and the French song plays, can you hear me I'm singing it? I want you to hear it, can you hear it? You've reached the portal and you go inside, you hesitate before entering. The boy watches you the while, your back is tight and drawing his attention and mine; your dress swirls around your knees. You might not love me anymore, I didn't mean to hurt you, I'm sorry that—Dear girl, can you imagine I'm listening to love songs on the radio? I want so much for your calves to wrap around my waist and hold me tightly and I want to bury my sex in your small enclosed sex and I want to obliterate you and beat you and fuck you—when can you come to me? Walk by me with the bowed back, your muscles tighten when you walk by me. When does Sunday arrive? Why is it that now after so many women and girls it is the servant girl of the pig-neighbor who inspires me to sing the French love song? Ah Juliana, we live together in this flat and we live in different places—your mind one place and mine another. One moment and I am sipping a cola drink at Uncle Sam's and you are my eye's delight; one moment I am holding you and there is no thing I want different and I tell you this and that and the shut-off box holes in my mind are not so large or precarious and do not pose the biggest betrayal; time is conceivably marked by my loosening belly and old skin on my face and I see a servant girl's nipples and I am undone, in one moment? The brown nipple loosely outlined by a faded white dress—not a breast, just the soft push of her teat. Ah Juliana, if I were a poet I would write the lyric to this girl's teat—is it possible that a round of flesh can so change a man? The old Armenian women drink their coffees in the afternoon and tell their stories of the Turks who sliced off the small loose breasts of the girls: what did they do with the conical huts? The artifacts of flesh they'd created? Armenia must be filled with our women's teats, did they pile them on high like sow ears and chicken feet? Or did they discover that it wasn't the breast itself, but the insinuation beneath the cloth, the heart beating and the breath moving the chest up and down and the soft protruding nipple also up and away from the soft cotton. The chopped breasts of no value, undesirable, loose from the body, with them you cannot even make soup.

I fell in love in that moment, like a man tossing over his balcony railing for the sea. Or: I came undone in that moment, like the same man upon impact. As you can see, it's quite easy to be a liar. There are few moments in a lifetime that can be sorted out and dusted off as the moment in time—not in the orphanage for boys and the Mairig holding up her cane; not at Uncle Sam's and you sipping the cola drink; and not in the pig-neighbor's house for apéritifs and Béatrice and her form. I look back now and I know I can't undo one act or emotion from the next, untangle the desire, the cruelty, the sadness and delight, and I try and precisely mark the moment to better understand my life, it would be meaningful to understand each moment like a mathematician solves each equation ('Ratiocination, boys!'). That boy, Vosto, did he do it? He was me, perhaps. I was the tortured boy, you've seen my scars? I slept alone. I crapped my pants. I was the fucked-one day after day. And you, Juliana, a figment of a boy's imagination? Leading me inevitably to love the young Palestinian servant girl? We are sacks of flesh, nothing more; we are detachable, detainable, *abandonné*. Juliana is working, I wonder if her feet are still bothering her? (my eyes close) everything is tinged green, as if seen through green glass, and we are at the swimming pool exactly as we were last night—and it is as if the day has not transpired, as if I haven't risen, worked, eaten my share and smoked and had my coffee and now for a lie down and thinking of Béatrice outside our lobby and Juliana and my eyes close: and I am back in last night's dream, exactly as if I had never left it. My eyes open: the blue sky is bluer than I can remember, the sun and the car horns are blazing, one loud blaring Fiat and my eyes snap open. What about Juliana? We are together at the poolside and I must get her some figs from the vendor but the vendor is not allowed into the pool area, it is for members only, and she wants those green figs more than anything, she is lying on the divan by the pool in her white bikini—she looks good, she has lost weight and she is thin all over. I walk outside the fenced area and I am on a thoroughfare, thousands of cars are blaring by me with their car horns and I see Béatrice across the street, she looks different, older and more beautiful, and my erection rising I think only that I must fuck her: I desire to fuck her. I find her and she turns around and smiles at me and I think: in this dream I will control the end, I can make things happen the way I like. She comes to the flat with me, her teeth are white and glossy like wet fruit. We climb the stairs, she is wearing a dress (hurry), into our room, get her clothes off, my penis into her sex—it is ecstasy but I cannot see her face, I feel her tight legs, I want only to come now: now.

I can make this happen, I am not so asleep. The Fiat is louder down below in the street and I am back on the balcony, close my eyes (hurry) put her back on the bed and me fucking her: but it's no use, I open my eyes and use my own hands. Béatrice has long since gone into the lobby with her purchases for Madame Yusef. Juliana will be home soon. I look at the clock to see the time on it.

XV

I am lying because I loved you love you and because, my darling, a lie can be closer to the truth.

XVI

I HAVE A PHOTOGRAPH taken by a German soldier during the Great War. The German took his photos during his military duty in the Orient and the photo is of a Kharphertsi boy, black and white, Ottoman Empire 1915. I found the reproduction in one of the Armenian journals (of which there are so many in Beirut) and its demands in bold letters that the demoniac race, confession, bear responsibility for the destruction and suffering of the Anatolian Armenian clans. In the photo the child is covered head to toe in rags, in layers of torn cotton and wools. His feet are bare and his hands are invisible beneath too long sleeves; his feet splay as if they have done much shoeless walking. The boy is looking into the camera lens and squinting from the sun's light; he is looking up at the German soldier who rises above him. For years I have carried this photograph in my billfold and occasionally I pull it out and stare back at the stare of the boy. I say 'he' for I have always thought him to be a boy, but it is impossible to ascertain the sex of this child; his sex is untellable from the photo, his name not knowable, he is rightly six or seven years old. I cannot remember the name of the journal where I cut the picture from years ago, or in what month or year I began carrying it in my billfold, but I am certain it is not me in the likeness. This is certain not only because the child is older than I am and we do not bear any resemblance to each other, but also because his look is one of sorrow and despair—he wears the mask of the orphan. He looks like an orphan, this boy whose mouth is opened slightly (his lips a beautiful gray) as if he were going to speak and what would a lost boy say to the foreigner? His look is the look of sadness—in this photograph I can see it. It is not the rags that tell of it, his stance with the bared knee slightly bent, or the invisible hands, I assume he has hands. What marks the public sadness for this boy? I think it is his look to the German, what he must have hoped for in the European soldier; he stopped walking or begging and stood still for the foreigner, looked up at him calmly— see me, he doesn't say, I am the sad boy. See me, there have been hands to caress this child's flesh and hands to cradle me and hands in the darkness, O he is a boy to have known sorrow. And he could very well have been my uncle, my mother's youngest cousin; we are kin in any case, kin made from an event in history. Not one moment, but many bound together and routed from hearths and bundled up in his raggy hat-turban—there is of course the moment of the photograph. I have no idea if the boy survived, if the photo marks an arrival somewhere or if he is still in the desert: if his bones have become part of the sanded landscape. The background of the photograph is blurred, only the boy's shadow is distinguishable behind him rising at a sharp angle like a tall building in the distance. He is a boy out of time, alone with his shadow, from an unknowable place and clan, and unlike me and unlike all of us (except the one) from the boy's orphanage, he is a sad boy, he misses what he has known, the heat of the hearth, the open orchard with the figs hanging low and the pomegranates dipping to the ground from too heavy boughs, the soft voice at night, a lullaby. He is not rude and bitter, he did not crush the boy's hand who took his bread, or beat the weak for their stupidity and their weakness. I love his sorrow and what I imagine to be a kind of chagrin, he has left childhood behind in the photograph, perhaps it marked the end for him, but still there is a discernible childlike look to him, a trace left in his look and lean and slightly parted lips. I have no photos in my possession from my time in the orphanage and so I cannot compare his photograph to mine. But I know we never had that look, the boys that were raised up in the Nest never wore the orphan's mask of sorrow and despair. We wouldn't have lasted out a week.

XVII

TODAY IS ONE of the summer days when it never cools, not even in the darkest hour of night, when the skin remains moist and sticky and the flesh is heavier and slow and it is too much to rise or to eat or move about the flat quietly. *Smoking, thinks:* when they walked through the Arabian desert, the heat turned their skins brown black green. Why can't you speak to me? I will go to the desert to find you. Here in this handful of dust. Here in this handful of dust. I am speaking to you but I am not certain of the listening (*one speaks, one notlistens*)—I would break through the thin barrier of the living and the dead to speak with you for a moment and ask you: your name, your village, and what I desire is your flesh. I am not so stupid, I know I can never get it back. I am not so interested in spirit as in your breast. What day and how did you perish? What parcel of earth holds your bones? These are not as important to me as: of what do you smell? Which breast hangs lower than the other? The shape of your legs, the bend in your arms, the marks, skin on your face and the dark vein beneath your eye—these are the things I would like to know. The map of your body, Mother. In your body I could find everything I need. The man who has no mother's form to form him is a sad man, unanchored man, vile and demoniac.

I am hot and sick today, all of my desire is to lie in bed but I am lying on the cracked tiles and I must sleep, I think, for a little while, until I am better able.

XVIII

I WALK AROUND in my mind like a man walks across an open field. I am slow and deliberate and watching my boots disappear into the sedge appear and then lift my eyes because it is raining now and the trees in the distance are moving swiftly because it is windy and I am slowly lifting my boots, careful, deliberate and everything is green in my mind and still I lose my footing, the man stumbles into a concealed grass-hole and I see the sea as I first glimpsed her as a small boy: the train passing through the tunnel, the turn round the bend of the mountains and the vast blue belt that stretched out in front of us boys, out into infinity beyond the train windows and the city at the base of the mountains. We strained against the windows, we pressed our faces to the glass, one of the boys yells out 'See the New Jerusalem!' and the train makes its descent toward the blue expanse marked on all sides by lighted bonnets. (We at first thought these white apparitions were thousands of the dead come to meet us, the martyrs from the old place, and when we could see that the blue was water, one of the boys yells out 'See they're Fish' and I imagined for many kilometers that the waters were filled to the brim like a closed barrel. As we made the final descent into the city the waves emerged from the sea, having been there always, my vision now making them into what they were.)

This picture of the sea, the sea when she was foreign to me, is the earliest picture I can find, I press into my mind but there is nothing before that descent into blue—I cannot remember the interior, the twin towns of Kharphert and Mezre in old Turkey, the train leaving the station in Eregli, the mule ride from Kharphert over land (for weeks) to Eregli; the boys' first trip on the metal moving machine. During our years of schooling at the Nest we were told the stories of before, of the boys from Kharphert orphanage, the Danish House, arrived in this place (the desert exodus, extracted fingernails, our fathers in piles). As for records there are none: I am Vahé or I am not and it is of no matter, the fruit is on the vine and it ripens and eat it up, be a good boy. As for the histories (the desert exodus, extracted fingernails, our fathers in piles) they are as foreign to me as any foreign country: my life began with the sea's panorama as the train wound its way down the mountains of the Lebanon into the city of Beirut. I press into my mind but there is nothing before that descent into blue, the rain abates, the wind is even now and the man walks on.

[You wanted one of your seven children to live; you loved them. Baba was killed already, they took him with the other men of Kharphert and burned him in the konak and bludgeoned him to death who cared to spend a bullet on an Armenian dog. You were acquainted with the Danish lady Miss Peterson at the orphanage and you gave over your boy and you did walk on. He cried when he was given over to the stranger and your scent and skin and your teat between his lips (your breast which made the world) were missing to him and he made a ruckus. You walked on with your clan toward the Der-el-Zor (you walked away from him and so the world). I don't imagine the instance of your death, Mother, and I don't oblige you, even in my imagination, to lament your seventh son. I am schooled in the dark hunger and I know it leaves the heart a dark and open field; in that place bargains are made, calculations of children are made, and you walk on, as I do, goodbye Vosto: here bread is more than blood.]

I am on a train moving down the desiccated mountainside to the city where I now live. My memory begins here, I can pinpoint the beginning of what I remember. A blue wall becomes the sea and then we are bathing in the seawater. Thousands of orphan boys are unloaded from the boxcars and running to the sea. It is so hot in the transport and it has been weeks since we've bathed properly. They unload us and *yalla!* they say, herding us down to the waters, hurry, remove your clothes, and without modesty there are thousands of us stripping to our bare skin, the newly bared skin is fair relief against the black and soot on our arms and feet and faces. We are thirsty from our days' journey and thousands of us running down the slope of warm sand into the welcome belly of the Mediterranean and drinking; we never knew the sea until this moment, and I remember that bitter surprise: the beautiful warm salt waters that made us spit and vomit.

I am floating naked in the seawater and then Vostanig is here, this way and that. I am in the first class at the orphanage in the Lebanon. The sea lies one hundred meters from our dormitory but we are barred from bathing or even walking along her shores;

there is a high fence to keep us from the water. We are never given reason for the fence, we are given the rules and we transgress or obey them. I can see the sea through the high chain fence and the sea breezes cool us or make us cold in the winter. I am in the first class and Vosto arrives at this place. It is nineteen and twenty-three and it is raining terribly. The boy was left outside the walls of the orphanage, in front of the administration building. He was deposited there in the middle of the night, by whom we were never to know, Vosto, as I have said, did not speak a word for many months and the first word, 'Mama', was spoken involuntarily during his sleep. I see Vosto, he is wet from the night spent in the rains. One of the mairigs is leading him into the compound, holding him gently (she was a nice one) and he allows himself to be led, you can see he is used to being led from here to there, something that would never change over the years. He is, of course, the ugliest boy. His hair is sparse and grows in patches, his body is covered in open sores. His ears loom large on a large head: all appears large on his head because his body is, by comparison, a bag of tied-up bones: his knees bigger than his legs, his arms hang at an awkward angle, you can count each rib, see each vertebra in his back, the collarbones and chestbones rise clear and high above the tight skin of his chest as if some horrible creature is trapped there and trying to push free. He comes to us shirtless, shoeless, head uncovered. All of this is perhaps unremarkable to the boys or to me in particular. Who didn't arrive shoeless, hatless, with hunger etched in the skin stretched tightly over the bones? His teeth so large in a looming face, his nose, teeth, ears seemingly larger than the whole of his child's body. What then is unusual about the picture of this boy Vostanig? The boy we soon enough called Kooskoos because he looked like a landed bird. Why do I remember the sea and then him looming in front of the orphanage walls? Him I hated, wanted to break apart. He came to us and was it the look of pity? Was it the look of sorrow and despair? Vosto never learned in all of his years with us to eradicate this look from his face and body. Even later when there was food enough for all of us and all of us filled out and went to bed satiated rather than to the accompaniment of our constant hunger. We beat him over and over, we punished him mercilessly, he lost his vision in the left eye, his arm was broken on one occasion, the Mairig took special pleasure in using him to demonstrate a broken rule. All of us tried, I think, to unmake his look of sorrow: the Mairig herself could not bear it. He was weak and he cried and I would have killed him then, he was fucked for this weakness, yet to his credit that boy in front of the red brick walls of the orphanage never gave it up and loved it in that place. I have said weakness, but perhaps it was his strange fortitude, because no matter the beatings and no matter the tauntings, Vostanig remained unchanged. The stranger: he was all of us, the damned exiled race in its puny and starved and pathetic scabbed body. How we longed to kill him.

It is said by some that the dead are ever returning to us in an unending cycle of vengeance and despair. I press into my mind as if to find them there. It is green then blue then rains. And they do come back to me, each one in his time.

XIX

I can still fuck it and the children grow in my belly not of my volition and my volition doesn't inhibit the seed its latching onto the walls of my womb and grows. I did not will it and they ate at my table uninvited and they are born into it with no other sense of themselves than sheep for the slaughterer, good laborers. Every year I bore a child (not of mine) and I can kill him because he can never be mine. This is how I do it (how is it that we can suffer and it keeps on, the sun moves across the sky and the halfmoon rises later that evening and the trees in early spring with the tight buds (beautiful) and it is hot today or it is not: it keeps on and it changes nothing, you can see sunlight); perhaps you never loved me. You hated my father because he made the child you didn't want, the bastard, the Muslim, the Turk he forced into your womb and created what you now hated. He killed your husband and your good boys and girls. He pushed your skirt up and tore your undergarments, you were screaming in the dead language (he heard your syllable-sounds like a sheepherder hears the latent ram) for Jesus and to your husband who lay dying. He twisted your legs and he loved fucking you, he'd had a hard-on for weeks during the military campaign. You were his first girl. The other soldiers in the infantry laughed and made jokes about his tenderheart for the infidel. The first weeks of the campaign and he vomited outside the perimeter of every village (the smell), 'you're a good boy,' the other soldiers told him and slapped him on the back. 'Watch and see how it's done.' He didn't look, he vomited outside each dwelling while his friends amused themselves inside (the smell). But today is different because (despite the vomiting) he has had a hard-on for weeks. He saw you and he grabbed you before his friends could grab you. They seemed surprised and clapped him on the shoulder. He wanted some privacy for his inauguration and he told his friends to wait outside. He slammed his fist into your face, you are screaming at him (Bua bua bua) and you fall onto the dirt floor; he has broken your front teeth and blood is spilling from your mouth. He sees your blood and kneels and pushes up your skirt and rips open your undergarments. You are screaming at him (Please please please) and scratching his face, you are able to scratch his face terribly. He hits you again and then again. You are screaming, now you don't; now you don't move you lie on the floor with your legs tightly closed, your pubic hair is visible and black, he holds your arms down at your side. The blood is bright on your lips and nose and I am aroused, like my father. Slap her, he slaps you. Force her legs open, he opens your legs and the ecstasy of it! Mother, he is fucking you and you scratch his face again and he slaps you again. Fuck her, and he does. (Bua bua bua) I am holding my cock now (it's hot today) my shirt is off and my trousers are open to my hips. His ass is moving up and away from your body and my hand is moving up and down my penis. You are arousing the both of us and I ejaculate and it is hot today and it's enough, there are no clouds that I can see from the balcony, the balcony rail cuts the sky into four pieces.

I don't like to kill her but I do what makes me

XX

HE COULD HAVE BEEN a better man, different from the man he was; and he could have been different, better than he is. In a different place he says I love yous and in that place he is a casanova and instead of the dream he doesn't wish to dream he has an island far out in the Mediterranean Sea, thousands of kilometers from any landmass and the nations and the clans sects rules confessions and he is standing there now. He is atop a knoll in the center of the island and he turns east then west and each way he turns he can see the water, from all of the vantage points he faces the sea—from the beginning it has been sea and sunlight, the light reflected throughout the corridors of the city and his thoughts making patterns like the patterns clouds make on the pavement and up the bâtiments as they race, crisscrossing the sun, cement. A light that illuminates everything: the corners of rooms and men's linen suits and the girls' black plaits to a light brown. The sea is at his back in the west and the sea is reflected in his face turned east, refracted by his pupils: the light takes him up and he floats at sea and lands on the knoll of this island, it is a small island in the middle of the Mediterranean Sea and thousands of kilometers from any landmass or the nations of massed clans. Here he isn't different from the man he became, a man made of war, but he is happy. He is a happy man alone on his small island and he is standing on the knoll in the center of the island and he is waving and his wave makes an arc like a lightning arc. The sea because she is honest and she is sadder than you know and more than dangerous. But at the last, in the moment before he is unable to think any longer (the moment before the boy who is holding a pistol to his neck and fires the gun and unmakes the thinking), he is sitting in his salon and it is nineteen and eighty-six and June and wars and hot today and he is looking toward the sea and he remembers when he first saw the sea as a boy of five on the transport from Kharphert overland to Eregli and then Eregli to Beirut via locomotive. They are coming out of the tunnel where it is dark and unlighted and in a moment (the moment before the boy with a red handkerchief tied round his head moves his index finger the requisite two centimeters, uses the force of his index finger) he sees the blue band stretching out before him and he thinks it is the New Jerusalem. And in a few kilometers the blue Jerusalem becomes the sea and forever afterward he thinks of her this way: the sea has always been a solace, his haven, and she is sadder than you know and dangerous; beautiful.

XXI

JULIANA GAVE THE NEIGHBOR three lira to borrow Béatrice for the Sunday meal. The little girl shows up at eight o'clock in the morning. She is slight with light brown hair and it is her eyes that are unusual, I notice her eyes when she comes onto the balcony with my coffee in her hand; she serves me my Sunday coffee, Sir here is your café, she says, I take it from her and go back to my newspaper; she has clear green eyes, the color of new leaves. I am reconstructing that moment: the lithe girl on our balcony handing me the small demitasse of coffee. Did I notice her that first time she was lent out to Juliana for the three lira? Not likely, but I see her now at eleven: she is wearing a faded polka-dotted dress passed to her by one of the neighbor's girl children, it is wrinkled at the hem and wet from the dishwashing. She has no breasts and her arms are thin and hang to her sides like sticks; her hair is bound in one long plait. I don't reply to the child and continue reading the daily. She helps Juliana all day with the cooking and later she will do all of the washing up, when the guests arrive she is handed their coats by Juliana, she awkwardly passes the apéritif plate around (and is mildly reprimanded for doing it awkwardly, No girl, one at a time, Juliana admonishes, the whiskey is for Mister and the sherry for Madame). At eleven o'clock that night she is sent home with a sealed envelope to be given to her employer for her services. Juliana perhaps gave the girl some caramels, the girl is delighted with them. 'Thank you, madame. Goodnight, madame.'

You have lived with that pig and his wife for how many years now, my darling? Five? Six? Tell me how long you have been cleaning their dishes and scrubbing their floors and whitening the diapers and the floors and the porcelain toilet while that pig's wife stands by, berating you pinching you, and you so small you had to use that step stool for years. I've seen you. The first time a few weeks ago, and now I am recalling all of the years you have been here since you were sent by your father from the south: a girl from the Sidon refugee camps—too many in your family to feed? now you feed them with your wage.

'Sir, Madame wants to know if you are still hungry?'

'No. Bring me the tobacco.'

'Sir, Madame would like to know if you are warm enough without your sweater. Here is your sweater.'

'Bring me whiskey and tobacco and tell Madame I am fine.'

'Yes, sir.'

WE'D BEEN INVITED to the pig's house for drinks, some occasion that Juliana felt it was important to honor. The pig is unhappy about the rising unemployment and unhappy about the rising costs of his daughters' tuition at the lyceé and hopes his commerce will increase and Béatrice is walking among us, filling our glasses, bringing the bowls of pistachios, pumpkin seeds, dried chickpeas. She hands me my drink, she is now approximately thirteen years old and her breasts are beginning to show. She is looking down when she gives me my whiskey, I can make out her dark nipples through the cloth of her faded white dress, they are protruding and I see the girl in front of me as more than the whiskey-bearer or the sweater-lofter: her nipples are soft and yet protrude boldly baldly like an unseen invitation, an interrogative of flesh: do the others see them or is it only me she invites unseen? The neighbor's daughters send the girl out of the salon and continue passing the foodstuffs. Their nipples hidden and bound up in their dark wools. They are clean-smelling and polite.

'COME HERE GIRL. Stand closer.' I stand up. It is Sunday and Juliana has gone out to buy a gâteau at Michel's. Béatrice has wandered out of the kitchen and into the salon. I walk up to her, today she has hidden her nipples from me. I would like to hold her against me and grab her from behind. 'How long do you work with Mr Yusef?'

'Pardon? Five years.'

'What's your age?'

'I am thirteen and a half year.'

'Your family, where do they live?'

'At Ein el-Helweh Camp in Sidon.'

'You born there?'

'Yes.'

'Where are they from?'

'Haifa.'

'You see them?'

'Yes, sir. My father comes to pick up my wage every three month.'

'You like your employ?'

'Yes, sir.'

'You are treated well?'

'Yes, sir.'

'My mistress, he treats you well?' (*alas, my continual confusion of 'he' and 'she' in Arabic*)

'Yes.'

'Thirteen, eh? You look to be ten, so slight you are. How long have you been coming here to help the mistress?'

'A while yet.'

'How long?'

'Almost three years.'

'Would you like a chocolate?'

'No, merci.'

'No, merci? Here, take it. I've bought these chocolates and I would like for you to take it.' She is still looking at the floor and I've grabbed her hand and push the gold box of truffles into her small hand.

'Merci.'

'Yes. Go make more coffee.'

That was the moment, wasn't it my dear? How your form undid a man such as me.

XXII

YES, it's hot today and *I failed to mention the salubrious details
and there were those, but in this instance that is not the case and my
failure to mention is no obfuscation or artifice but rather it is that the
words themselves were not prepared for the saying and until they
could be said they were unsayable and so I forgot them and because of
it failed to mention the insalubrious detail which is now remembered
and sayable now and so I say it, said: Jumba was not right. He did
not fulfill his obligations and the expectations put upon him as upon
all of us, the animal and the man alike, and the animal in his cage
(and the man) also. Because as the male he ought to have, and thus
being obliged to do it, and as Ali said to me from the first he is not
right, he is a chimp who turns his ass when the female bares her canines. And when I saw Jumba I saw him sitting behind her until she is
finished eating and he grooms her hour after hour, he pushes his long-
fingered paws into her sex and he arouses her to orgasm (and she
doesn't return the favor on his red and wanting prick). He was a big
chimpy, he must have weighed in at fifty kilo and Urakayee was*

smaller and fifteen kilo smaller and he could have been right with her (perhaps with the others that died before I began my weekly visits he could not have done it because of their size and belligerence and so, but with the smallish Urakayee?) Ali said from the beginning that that one is not right and whoever heard of an ass-giving bull? So an aberration of nature. He doesn't return her screams or peel back his lips and show up his canines but his hair stands on end and he is running away and yelling out and he is taking the shit because he is shitting and running and he is throwing it shitting and wiping his shit in his black coat while he is running away and then he doesn't stop her her canine diversions into his flesh when she's reached him and he's all shat up and cowers and the biting and doesn't stop or try to but only running away or quiet as she does it until he is bleeding and then scarred on his head and torso. Why does he do it, make himself into that? Because we called Vosto the 'Ass-giver' in the orphanage, and that I forgot until this very moment, in this moment I remember that we called him that, and he bent over at the waist and Garo with his big prong at thirteen would stuff it up there. The fucked one, the female boy, weakling—we shoved our sex into his ass and it was pleasure beyond any other we could find, the queue of boys stretched behind the bunkhouse, ten to fifteen, the older boys first and then the younger (dominant) boys and even the boys who were too young still and couldn't make milk but loved the sensation of cock in that girl's 'pussy.' Now that I remember it and it is sayable I can say it and the saying arouses me. And there are other things to say because of the necessity of their saying, first I can see them and then say them, or sometimes I first say and then see, say this: all war is deception as is all history.

XXIII

—Monsieur, you like your shoes shine?

—How much?

—Twenty-five piastres.

—Go ahead.

—You like them shiny?

—Yes.

—I'm Vosto.

—Pardon?

—Vostanig Egoyan. You remember? From the Nest from the old days.

—No.

—Monsieur Vahé Tchuebjian.

—No not me.

—Yes it's you, monsieur. We were compatriots.

—Not me, the wrong man.

—You don't remember the wine we took from the rectory? How the Mairig wanted to get us then! And the paper horses you'd make and we'd trade them for the pencil nubbins. What happened to her I wonder, that ugly bitch, uglier than me even. Do you hear me, Monsieur Vahé? Okay? (ha ha ha) Now we could pay her back with our strong bodies, but then one look from her, no was all it took from her, and the worst of it

(*not me not me not me*)

was we did love her, didn't we?

(*not me not me not me*)

Like a dog loves the master who kicks him and throws him the table scrap (ha ha ha). Well, we made it, didn't we? Didn't we, Monsieur Vahé? We made it good.

—(*not me not me not me*) Take it.

—Merci. It is good to see you. I'm Vosto, remember: it's good (ha ha ha). Excuse these black hands. Until next time.

—Yes, goodbye.

XXIV

These are the lies:

1. Vosto
2. That is not how it happened
3. My age
4. I smoke too much
5. It's hot today

Some facts:

1. There are 17 official confessions in Lebanon:

    Baha'is:

    Christians:

    Armenian Catholic

    Armenian Orthodox

    Armenian Protestant

    Greek Catholic

    Greek Orthodox

Latin
Maronite
Nestorian Assyrian
Nestorian Chaldean
Protestant
Roman Catholic
Syrian Orthodox
Druze:
Jews:
Muslims:
Shi'ia
Sunni

2. The Ottoman Empire ruled the Lebanon and Greater Syria until the end of the First World War; and in 1920, the French (consulting with the Maronites) made *Liban*: Beirut, Tyre, Sidon, Tripoli; the Lebanon and Anti-Lebanon mountains; the Beka'a Valley; made a Christian dominated state

3. in the East; and in 1943 (Lebanon declares independence and) the one Maronite and the one Sunni make a pact, it was not written, made the National Covenant— *"and the Maronites will cease identifying with the West and in return the Muslims will respect the integrity of Lebanon and prevent its merging with any other Arab state.*

4. *Public offices should be distributed proportionally among the recognized religious groups, and the president of the republic*

will always be Maronite; the prime minister Sunni; and the speaker of the Assembly Shi'ia. The ratio of deputies will be 6 Christians to 5 Muslims"—made the state confessional.

5. <u>See</u> your confession on your "Carte Nationale d'Identité du Liban"—because: in Lebanon blood does not change to water; because: here in the Lebanon you cannot marry or divorce or bury the dead without the abetment of your church, your mosque, your temple; and

6. *I have a Carte Nationale d'Identité du Liban*: (the Armenian Christian refugees given them in 1924 by the French):

Nom: Tcheubjian	Domicile: 55 Rue Makdissi 4e B Ras Beyrouth
Prénom: Valié	District: 20
Nom du père: inconnu	Sexe: M
Nom de la mère: inconnu	Taille: 1 m 57
Né le: 26 September 1917 à: Turquie	Poids: 73 kilo
Religion: Orthodoxe Arménienne	Yeux: marron
Métier: charpentier	Cheveux: châtain
Situation de famille: marié	Miscellanées: menteur connu

a photo

7. This is a photograph of the boys from the Bird's Nest Orphanage. It was sent to America.

Nous sommes bien obligés envers les Americains parce qu'ils nous aident toujours. We are grateful for the help of America.

I could be the boy in the second row, seven in from the right.

BOOK II

I

THEY ARE NAKED like Adam and they run to the sea's edge. They say for shame and they drink the Mediterranean waters as if it were Christ's blood and it does not quench and they gag, a gaggle of boys running for the sea and knowing only the waters of the interior: these boys of the time before; before salt waters and their testicles rose with the salted waters and they bounced on the waves and they prayed for the progeny of the race. They prayed for a miracle, a name, to remember their tongue, the tongue they'd left them, the tongue they didn't remove; the hands, a heart, a boy's untold things. And they are no longer dreamers, Adams in the wasteland: they till the soil, its thorns and thistles; they eat the bread made from the sweat of their brow: they are Adams, cast off, castoffs, in the sea and by the sea's edge, they unload them from the boxcars, the cattle cars, they remove their clothes and yell *yalla* and they run, these boys, to the sea to the waters and they drink as if it were Christ's redemption and they gag, they cannot speak, the thorn and thistle is in their throat—untold boys, they are from the time before and no longer dreamers. Now they are Adams in the wasteland.

II

SUNDAY, MAY 17, 1964   THE DAILY STAR—BEIRUT, LEBANON
Comparison of Ape-Men and Gorilla Brains

CAPE TOWN (R)

—Dr. P. V. Tobias, professor of anatomy at the University of Witwatersrand's Medical School, said here today that fossil ape-men had no bigger brain capacity than the gorilla, but it enabled them to use tools and probably also to fashion them.

Dr. Tobias was addressing the diamond jubilee Congress of the South African Association for the Advancement of Science on the brain capacity of Zinjanthropus, the fossil ape-man found in Olduvai Gorge, Tanganyika, three years ago by British anthropologist Dr. Leakey.

Dr. Tobias said his analysis had shown that however manlike fossil ape-men were in other respects, in their cranial capacity and therefore presumably their brain size, they showed no substantial difference from gorillas.

«It may be stated that the brains of both gracile and robust forms, undoubtedly conferred on their owners the ability to use tools and probably also to fashion them,» he added.

III

BECAUSE IT WAS IN ERROR all of it: god, the tools, the mind, the hands. Because it has only led to this: is there anything else but the infliction of pain and he suffers it? Jumba taught me this. It was me who took the photographs of him, the pitiful beast. I gave him the cigarettes and he took my burns as payment for them. He approached me slowly, his neck chain drags, he comes and knows first the pain and then the pleasure. Jumba loved me hated me and the pain and the pleasure. And in the end, I made the end for him pleasurable. It was a beautiful sunny spring day. There were no clouds in the sky, it was one of the days when the Mediterranean sun lights up every inch of the city—you couldn't find your shadow on such a day. I rose early in the morning and dressed carefully, my suit was pressed and my shirt. I left the apartment before the churchgoers and I made a stop at the bakery and the baker opened his doors early so that I could make my purchase and I made my way up Rue Sadat and Rue Danant passing the gate and the garden and Ali saw me at the entrance and waved me in as usual and the bust of Monsieur Marnier greeted me and I carried my parcel underneath my arm and my too long toes scratched in my shoes and I made my way past the aviary house and past the sick house and I saw Jumba in the distance in his cage, he'd just been let out of the night-house. He saw me and smiled, lifted his hand waving. I sat on the bench by his cage and lighted my cigarette and he approached me and I did it I pressed the burning embers into his flesh and then handed him the cigarette and gave him the pastry and he took it and ate it and smoked his cigarette looking up through the bars past the old hanging tire eating and smoking and I was thinking how pleasant it would be to share a meal with him. I saved Jumba that day—released him from his cell with a gâteau from Michel's and the poison—powdered sugar coating the top of it. I remained by his side for hours that morning and soon enough I found him with his hands resting on his belly, his chin resting on this chest. Beatific. Jumba at peace. I loved him made him happy.

IV

WHEN THE MAIRIG announces the bath day we bemoan our
fate, the wait on line, the hard scrubbing and the steam and hot
water and then cold when there is no more hot; the harsh hands
of the mairigs. And for what, we want to know. To later then return to our barracks cold and disheartened by the harsh hands
that removed our small and fierce screens, the thin walls around
skin and the glass we carried around our hearts. They took it
away with their water and loofah and hands, the soap cakes, they
came onto our bodies and took from us some of what we'd
greedily hoarded (the locked soot and old wax and urine screens
and pieces of ourselves; dried wind and salt).

She was unbeautiful.

Miss Taline sits on a low stool in front of the bathing tub.
There are five tubs spread out in rows and the four other misses
and she. We are standing on line and now fighting for her queue
and she is there and unbeautiful, too thin and sad long face for
beauty (the rumors of killed children and husband and mother

and all in old Turkey) and the boy in front of her hands you can see on his face that it is ecstasy, the smallest and unexpected moment of grace behind the walls and in front of the Miss's dark hands, cut nails, long and sad face. The boy is closing his eyes and her hands are up his arms with the loofah and over the shoulders and the spine and buttocks and he can't hide from us, we stand on line and push into and then pushed out of her queue when the Mairig looks off: please, the eyes say before he closes them. Please, don't stop it. In and out of the queue and then toward the front a few of us make it into her hands (the others pushed into Miss Zabelle or Miss Azniv) and I am there and naked (the piles of underwear in a heap outside the doorway) and she lifts the tin of water high and spills it over me and the soap cake and the loofah up my arm and down to the base of the spine, the dip there, the lower legs, the heel. The boys look at me, at the look of grace, at Miss Taline's deep slide up my arms and behind the nape and the pause at the base of the spine. It looks like tenderness? We turned our sly cheeks from the kisses we didn't receive, we bruised the skin and his, we laughed out loud, we ran too much, we were loud and breaking too much, and trading items from our boxes (knucklebone, walnut hulls, glass buttons, a razor blade, twine) and lying and scheming and it was fun and we were schools of boys, in packs, we ran, we played knucklebones, played marbles, bartered and gambled with the lot of it— the boys are fighting, the Mairig yells at us to shut it, the cane is swinging loose down onto our heads, and above this the few moments of that lady's hands, naked and I am cold, and she is unbeautiful and they are different, long and sad (rumored) and then tender and then tender. The mairig Miss Taline, I recall not her comeliness (unbeautiful), but she is lovely nevertheless, she opened space on my skin and made the body mine, touchable, touch me, I am saying it still: please don't stop it.

BECAUSE I SAW HER TODAY. I am standing by Hamra and it is midmorning and cold because the winds are cold in November and so the only celebration we make for the season is at the arrival of the chestnut roaster with his portable stovepipe and newspaper cones and hot sweet fruits. I hand him the one-lira note and above his bent head see her walking toward me; she holds the hand of a small boy and walks briskly, going somewhere, arriving there; he hands me the cone of roasted chestnuts, they are crackled and brownblack, gives me my change and bewells. She walks past me and the boy asks for chestnuts as they pass and she says no they cannot, they must hurry (in the dead tongue) then *yalla*, please Nene, the boy urges and she tugs him on (he cries back to her for the halfburned winter nuts and she continues (dead): 'We don't buy from these people, not from the streets, the Muslims') and looks up at me and at the chestnut roaster and is perhaps slightly embarrassed and chagrined by her grandson's whining in the unintelligible dead way and so it is for this reason, I think later, that she doesn't see me. She sees a man in a slightly worn three-piece suit and shined loafers holds a cone of chestnuts, his hair brushed back and perfect with pomade and then the beginning gray in his hair and the beginning puckered skin beneath his eyes and large ears and doesn't see: a boy waiting on line hoping—for this more than for hard candy or faster runs or new shoes, in this moment wanting only to gain her station for the moment of the washing up and willing any connivance or stealth or trickery to get it. He pushes the boy ahead of him and trips the boy to his left. He pinches the boy ahead behind to the left of him, all of it to get at her bathing station. Did she see it then? He sees an old woman, rounded at the shoulders so that in ten years she'll be stooped and she completely gray-haired (an early graying, he thinks) and rumpled dress and one-inch-heeled shoes and a scarf tied round her neck and notbeautiful and he cannot help himself, he looks for the hands, at the hand that holds the boy's and recognizes her face not the hands and thinks how small she is, how unnoticeable, and doesn't wish to be the boy held by her hand and guided down the sidewalk toward the Corniche and sea and denied the hot chestnuts because of the impropriety of street chestnut sellers. 'Armenian?' the chestnut roaster asks and looks at him strange and he is not sure if he's been interrogated or if he's made the question and too afraid (I'm in a hurry also, thinks) to press and continues on his way (salaam as he leaves) to the market to buy: milk, chickpeas, rice and chicken. And she doesn't recognize me, he thinks, as he walks home from the market with his sacks of food: doesn't see anything in the man and she's old now and small and small hands and unable to take hold of him. She cannot do it anymore: touch him or bathe and he remembers her and then works to strike it and he cannot because she now like a diaphanous moving picture, runs over and over again and he unable to stop it or start it, a beast in his breast emerges because his chest is constricted and he breathes quickly and his organs tight and if he could just stop the moving picture he thinks he could get the beast out of his chest and ballooning organs and: doesn't think: *abandonné and abandoning abandonné*

and abandoning abandonné and abandoning abandonné and aban-
doning abandonné and abandoning abandonné and abandoning aban-
donné and abandoning abandonné and abandoning: hurries home
because it's late and Juliana needs the chicken for the midday
meal and thinks that if he can stop it he'll get the beast out and
can't stop it over the midday meal and coffees and a lay down afterward and it's there still pushing like a millstone pulling him on
to some kind of thought he would not like to think. I won't think
it, thinks: I will not.

V

OR IT WAS LIKE THIS: we are in a cave and it is night, in other places the jasmine and wisteria bloom. It is late summer of that year and we are cold at night. There are hundreds of us, the living and the notliving alike, a small lame girl holds a neonate to her chest and sings to him softly; he is inutterably quiet (he stopped crying days before) and she's given him a name: 'Here you will be Vahé' and she is comforted by the uncrying baby his name and doesn't think (of bread, tinned honey, new white cheese) about her mama and her auntie and the baby in the girl's arms is not me because I am sitting next to you in the cave, a beautiful boy who is not yet two years old and my brothers and sisters departed (lying sitting behind us on the roads and notroads) except for a five-year-old sister who has made it with us; you hold our hands fiercely; you say to yourself that you will keep the two of us, that the others have gone, yes, but these two will remain. We are naked in the cave, it is hot during the long days of walk and walk but now, at night, and unprotected and tired and the aches and bleeding cuts and bruised at the skull and the children are crying in the cave: *choor choor:* we want a little bit of water, Mama: can't you (why don't you?) give us the water and a piece of bread? we are cold.

You are holding my hand. I am a beautiful boy and I rest my head on your lap and you lift your limp titty and offer it to me and I try for the milk but there has not been milk in many months, but the suckling mother comforts me and I am comforted by your arms around me and your teat in my mouth (your chest bones extrude like a strange and sad harness, my cheek against the hard comfort). We don't like to sit next to the corpse but we do; the night is dark and cold and the policemen sitting outside the entrance to the cave and eat their dinner and rub their trouser legs and (their rifles slung across their backs) soon they'll come in for the girls and the girls in the cave are rubbing (more) dirt onto their cheeks, ripping their hairs apart, scratching their faces: good unbeautiful girls they have removed their teeth with stones. We sit and the lame girl sings Նորից զարուն եկավ, զարուն աննըմման and the Turkish women arrive at the entrance to the cave and they wear the black veil and they walk in (a Hello Effendi to the guards) and because they are piteous they whisper, 'Which of the brats will you sell?' and you are thinking, Mother, about the four or five you've already lost to the roads and notroads and the bayonet and you know that there are days and months left for it and that the Der-el-Zor is inexorable and terrible and it will never end and we will always be here in this cave without Him or anyone to save us and so you rise (the women as black hawks saying: 'Infidel, do you have any to sell?' the little girl sings on and on in that infernal lame voice in that dead language that doesn't save us) and you hold my hand and my sister's hand and she knows and cries to you to keep her and 'Mama I don't want to go' and 'You mustn't sell me. Please' and because I have no sentences and (prelingual) because she is saying it loudly in the already dead words and the old men are crying into their hands, you push her behind you and lift me up and lick my cheeks and lick the dried snot and dirt and I am cleaner around my nose and mouth and you give me over to one of them and the one takes me and throws the coin at your feet and old men and my sister? also and *voch*, *voch*, *voch* behind you and the lame girl cries, she is no longer singing it, and holds the uncrying neonate and me Mama: I was uncrying also but looking up at you as the one of them who is holding me says (she is backing out of the cave) in their tongue, the victor's tongue: 'Only a dog sells her progeny; Hello Effendi!; Yes yes yes; I'll call him   Mustafa.' The dog-bones fill the desert; the dead tongues; the no's of them in the nowdead tongues.

Perhaps it was this (last) looking at you that though forgotten made a picture in my mind and perhaps I took it then and I am still seeking this picture, walking around in my mind and slipping and falling but nothing before the blue, no body, just this swath of sea: blue and blue and blue. I don't want the (dead) words, only the picture: it would be enough. Or your bones, or your bones sifted out.

VI

I ALWAYS KNEW IT of course that to love you like I have, a middle-aged man with a paunch belly and the wrong words in your language ('he' when I mean to say: *you see darling in Armenian we have neither 'he' nor 'she,' no gender subject (only the dead subject)*: 'she'), the funny-talk accent in Arabic, the long scuffed toes, the wrinkles, dirty breath, not your confession, or your god, an Armenian man and all of it was ridiculous, beyond ridicule into the world of carnival and I am dressed in the suit of the beast, I have a proboscis and I can eat pistachio nuts and I sit in my cage and wait for you, my beautiful darling, before we must give up meat and sins of the flesh, but I could not stop it, could not make it stop, this internal organ's needs, desires, must have you: I desired you more than I have desired any thing or woman or boy in many a year, perhaps in a lifetime. I wanted you like that boy from the Nest wanted a Sunday sweetie; like he wanted more fatty soup; like he wanted warm days hot hands and hot baths and shoes and button shirts and color books and hush and—it was impossible darling because I could not have you, could not do it, because you could never see me, never see the internal organ me (salt warm sad) and I could not smell your cunt kiss you cradle your body in my hands and hold you on my lap, you are bent over my arm and your unbound hair drops to the floor in a rush and I would kiss it there, your cunt, and carry your smell on my lips and my fingers and rub your excrement in my hair and I would smell you on my fingers for days; my cunty hands would make tables and kitchen cabinets and long hollow boxes and there could be nothing more beautiful and I would swim in the sea but then I would lose you from my hands and lips so I'll not swim, I'll not bathe, I'll walk along the Corniche late at night and take my hand from my pocket and light a cigarette and the tobacco and you in my mouth, I suck on my fingers to remember—it is you Béatrice—not a Rita from behind the Banque Suisse, not that, no; and so he waits (here on my back, the broken tiles pushing through and making relief on my naked back). The out-of-place, unclanned boy, not of the race for the Palestinian girl; 'Mohammedan,' Madame Yusef says to us when you have returned to the kitchen, 'they're not part of our Lebanon'; the out-of-place girl (sans une carte d'identité) and without it and without knowing: meet me in the zoological gardens, pass beneath the sign, it reads: *Jardin Zoologique de Beyrouth* and then below in your language also. Read the sign and enter the gates and I will await you in front of the primate house, it is empty now, emptied of animal and dung and hay and perhaps awaits us, my darling, perhaps we can rest, ease ourselves there, we'll have a cigarette—would you enjoy a cigarette?—we'll eat a sweetie and rest there. I am tired today and it is hot and I could only ever love you more; I could only ever be more in love.

VII

AT KOKO'S PARTY we were introduced again, we had met once before at the Azadamard Club and you had forgotten my name by the time Koko pulled you over to me and told you my name and you didn't seem too concerned, you were having a glass of red wine and there was Western music playing loudly on the radio, you smiled and we discussed a radio show, the new film, Koko's funny jokes and who can remember such conversations now? Many months later you told me of your mother's work in the orphanage in Aleppo, your father's death of meningitis when you were a girl and your uncle who supported the idea of your studying in secretarial school; and I could have loved you, darling, I imagined that I could do it: a solemn man of no bearing, a good carpenter-man, and the Armenian girl who lives in Ashrafiyeh behind the Azadamard Club and she studies and becomes a secretary in the new government Office of Education. If perhaps our life together had not comprised the duty and obligations of inviting the friends, hoisting the image of the couple, worrying over the unborn child and trying to bear him to no end; if perhaps there was no such thing as habit and fatigue and responsibility and inertia and boredom and the need for more money and the customs between men and women, and the brothel; if perhaps I hadn't become accustomed to your hands your form as I sat on the balcony swing in the mornings and you served me my coffee manaish lebne; if perhaps the rough edges of your feet remained unknown to me, the untucked flesh, unrestrained and marked skin, your body's odors and your body without adornment, vulnerable and unprepared; if perhaps—then our covenant (like the National Covenant)—mythic, tenable, allied? Juliana, you did all of the things a good woman will do—the cookclean things, hostess for the invitee, the shop the barter the watch your form and ignore the sweeties—all of this you did well, you erased the past from your voice, you smoothed your skin with expensive creams, you removed the hairs from your limbs, the high heels, the tight jacket, tight coiffure, and it was never enough, my darling, was it, to make us different, better than who we were?

When we made love we never made love. Not that first time when you came to my flat, you were so beautiful that day and on many others. It was not the act of us together sans vêtements which made the love, but yes it made the pleasure. You crossed the room in your blue cotton dress and small-heeled shoes, your hair was pulled back and the makeup was not covering your face: there was a beautiful darkness cupping your eyes. You were timid that day in a manner I was not accustomed to with you. You, Juliana, the girl who defied her mother and went to secretarial school at night while supporting herself by day in Madame

Lemy's couture shop, you sewed suit after suit for the elegant ladies of Hamra. Never timid, never mind, not shy. You tightened the seams on your clothes, you made skirts and suit jackets and you walked across my room, I turned and looked at you and I could see you were afraid. For many years I had been a client downtown, my preferred locale near the Cinema Rivoli, the bordello with its Ritas and its red-tiled roof adjacent to the modern building never incongruous in our halcyon Beirut. I could see you weren't sure if you should remove your clothes or I and I wanted to play the casanova for you, I understood how it would ease things between us, so I kissed your cheeks and your neck. I was feeling a bit lazy too, thinking how Mr Casanova had much patience and correct words, 'Darling you are the most beautiful and Darling I love you and Darling is there any other woman as lovely as you? Oui, je t'aime.' I opened the buttons on your dress, I wanted a cigarette and when you were naked before me, your breasts looser, and the smaller one pointed, the thick finger nipples, than I had imagined in the many months we had been dating, I was aroused and part of me wishing it could be done quickly, the fucking unprescribed by the films you'd seen and other nonsense; I kissed your body and you were scared and I could not smell your arousal. Finally I decided we ought to fuck it and that you would get over the stories you had made in your mind, although we didn't speak of these stories. I removed my trousers and my cotton shirt and I felt your sex and put my finger in your sex and you were shocked, saying my name, and then does it matter? The usual man heaving onto the woman, I opened your legs wider and you were in pain although you said nothing while we did it. I admit that for me it was pleasurable, even enhanced by your pain and discomfort and I could or could not be a casanova and still, darling, I could fuck you. And although I could tell that the act disappointed you, I said, Okay?, and you were silent. The blood on my penis was red on my penis. You didn't see it or look at my sex before or afterward. You were dressing soon enough and you wondered if your difference would be showable in the mirror, you asked me and I embraced you. I had no particular desire for marriage then, but I understood, as did you, that despite our claims for modernness, our communal fate was fait accompli: we would marry in our mother church. And I wondered what Mr Casanova would say now, I put my arms around you: 'It was lovely, like you are lovely, Juliana. Parfait. Je t'aime.' I spoke the French you liked so well, the language that made the expensive creams and suit tailoring, that made us different to ourselves, how we longed for the distance, the dif-férence. To be modern, you said, not the dirty Arab carter in the dirty street yelling out his profanities and threats to kill the truck driver who toppled his cart and the truck driver's family; the refugee Palestinian mothers sitting on the street corners with their hands extended, dirty, saying: can't you (*why don't you?*) give us a piece of bread?; the car horns blaring night and day in this city.

I said, 'Okay? Ça va bien?' and you nodded and we left in the afternoon, the windows to my flat were left open. The sun was high above my building. I remember that you remembered it differently. Perhaps you told me of this many years later. Perhaps the sun was not high above the building and it was late in the evening, the foreign tongue insignificant, my finger in your sex unutterable, the car horns blaring night and day.

VIII

—Merci.

—A drink? We could have some arak. Darling, would you like some arak?

—Yes, merci. Lovely.

— You look lovely today, Rita. Your hair.

—Yes, I've had it washed and pressed at the new place.

—The new one?

—It's fantastic. Thank you, it's quite nice, strong. And so, your work—

—Fine. Yes I bought this last week when we drove to the Beka'a. Still the best producer in the Lebanon.

—The best.

—Come sit here next to me. It was your first time at the salon? What's it called?

—Yes, the first. I noticed it last week and, well, made an appointment on my way home. It was time for a change and it is chic and the sinks are beautiful inside and the chairs. Vahé. Okay, okay. Vahé, do you like it?

—Yes, darling. What time today?

—Yes I must leave no later than quarter past four. Okay, okay. Today I must not be late. No, I must be on time to pick up the boys. Otherwise

—Yes.

—Otherwise, you understand I must leave at a quarter past four and not late either. And my hair, I must be careful with my hair, I told my mother-in-law I was going first to have it styled and then to search out the new cloth and then to get the boys. Careful. Vahé. Okay, okay. Yes, let's go into the other room. My drink? No, I'll finish it here. It was good, strong though, don't you think? I would like to drive over the mountains to the Beka'a, perhaps go to the festival at Ba'albeck this summer and perhaps Om Koulsoum will perform again this year and Ibrahim and I never leave the city except to visit his uncles in the north. It's horrible. Have I told you? It's backward and I'm afraid to drink the water! I tell the boys: be careful, wash your hands, no don't eat that. I swear that after each visit I've got the dysentery. I tell the boys, don't act like them. Because after two days they begin to act like their village cousins and they are wild and unmannered and when I complain to Ibrahim he becomes angry with me. Why don't we go someplace new, I tell him, rent an apartment in Aley or Broumana with the boys? He doesn't listen to me. Always to his uncle's place. It's backward and yes, yes. Okay, okay. And not late either. I must pick the boys up on time. I told my mother-in-law my hair and then the cloth. I'll sit up, okay? Like so. Like so? Do you like it? It's called Martin after the owner, he studied hair in Paris for three years. He says that in Paris the women will bring their dogs into the salon. Have you been there? I would like to go and to go shopping for cloth and other things. Martin is shorter than me, he is a very short man even for a Jew. I told Ibrahim, let's save our money and go to France and he tells me Rita you are a stupid bitch and when he talks to me like that I am quiet but I ignore him at mealtimes so he gets it back. I think it would be nice to get a small dog, but they are expensive, the small ones? Vahé, do you listen?

IX

AND THIS ALSO TRUE: that you could never do it, that it was
not possible, as if one tried to measure the distance from here to
the blue dark line of the horizon—it forever beyond our reach
and like unheld water, wind, like the return of history or the unhistoried man, like the specters speaking and returning speaking:
c'était impossible. Because, my darling, you also could not see
me. See the middle-aged man with the growing paunch; see the
lifted hand shaking the tumbler from side to side because he
would like more whiskey; see the wrinkles, the lust, the hahaha at
the dinner parties; see the Armenian, the cigar in his mouth, the
cigarettes lighted one after another, he is clapping his hands together when the neighbor's girls sing the before-bed songs and
they are dancing in front of all of the guests, singing dancing and
twirling around and you give him his whiskey and hahaha everyone applauds the young clean neighbor's girls; he applauds and
takes the drink from you and sees the bruises on your arm when
the sleeves of your dress fall back from your wrists, looks up into

your face, not laughs, then you don't look at him, you straighten your back and you move away and the sleeves fall back into place and with the silver tray in your hand proceed to the next guest with his whiskey or arak. You don't look, cannot see: (salt warm sad): a lonely man who walks to the zoological gardens, makes cabinets and boxes, walks along the Corniche in the late evening and makes histories for his undead mother (undead because not lived)—he longs for her, for what he cannot know. And you could never do it, never love this man because you cannot see him; see: crooked teeth; tobacco on his breath when you lean over to give him his whiskey; small hands; lust in his eyes; hahaha with the neighbor and his wife and the other guests. —Not: (salt warm sad)—a man undone by history, unhistoried by it (like you?)

Or simply, darling, in sooth: because he is too old ugly smells old and you want a young strong man with big hands and a white even smile who loves you and sings to you and carries your packages and says 'You are the most beautiful' and 'Your eyes are like stars' and 'I cannot live without you, darling. I'll die without you.' The grocer's boy. The beautiful strong and lean boy who carries the boxes of rice and tinned milk and vermicelli to Yusef's flat. You unload the crates while he drinks the lemonade in the kitchen. He watches as you step up and down from your step stool, now not to reach the sink but to reach the highest cabinets to put away the rice and vermicelli noodles and he watching finally says your name and you turn to look at him, not realizing that he knew your name, and you smile at him, your calves taut from the stretch to put away the rice and noodles and he smiles in return. 'Do you like to go to the cinema?' he asks. And you cannot respond because then he will know that you have been to the cinema only one time and that you would very much like to go again and so you say nothing and he smiles again and says he will take you soon and he departs, puts his glass on the countertop and leaves through the servant door.

Does anyone suspect your affaire de coeur? Perhaps even you don't suspect it. Because you are a good girl and a strict girl. You are clean and organized and you press your dresses and your undergarments just as you press the girls' dresses and undergarments: you are even fastidious, strict with yourself, your nails cut short, your pots shine from the scouring, the floors, the glasses, the torn hems always repaired, your hair tied back in one long and even plait—everything in your domain is clean and sharp and strictly placed in rows, in piles, folded in two. You cannot understand the girls—their laziness, their clothes in a heap, they bicker and stain their dresses and Madame Yusef plaits their hair, checks their nails for them or you do it: because they are lazy, they complain and bicker with one another, they would like more and more and you, my darling, would like only one or two small things such as to go to the cinema on Sunday afternoon or a new polka-dot dress which is all the fashion these days or to return to Sidon and kiss your mother and put your arm through hers and walk down the dirt roads together at dusk. What else might you have wanted, darling?

X

I MISS JUMBA like the indulged vagrant child misses his best
wind-up toy and it broken now beyond repair by his own hands
which in a rage threw it across the salon and yells to his mother to
fix it fix it and she cannot and beats him for the carelessness and
waste and asks why do you curry what you love? And Jumba
sired two children before his demise and before Urakayee's de
mise (the pushed-forth cranium freed no less) and before she did
that she demised her boy Vahé. C'est vrai: the staff named the
boy Vahé, out of a sense of gratitude (I had begun to give small
sums of money to the Zoological Society) or as a small joke between themselves and the weekly visitor to the zoo. In any case:
she killed her boy who was their second child, the first having
been sold off to a traveling show in the Jordan years before I began my weekly visits. Of course the beast didn't love her children, a fucking monkey!, who like any beast, liked to fuck it. She
and Jumba were always doing it, he is sitting in the corner (this
before he is permanently chained) and begins to gesticulate and

irritate and rubs himself and turgid big sexual organ and red and he gets up and walks toward Urakayee who is drinking water and picks her nose and gets up and she turns her back to him (sees him coming, wants him to do it) he mounts her like a beast and the men liked to watch them because after she gave birth the first time she didn't understand how to mama her baby and so Ali told me they had to take the baby (a girl, Sukhari) out of the cage because it was dying of malnutrition and rough holds. The monkey didn't know what to do for the baby so the keepers took her (sold her) and then animal instinct to care for the young? But indeed, the second child, the boy child. The keepers had planned to remove the babe after it was born, as they had with the girl baby. They left Urakayee alone to labor through the night when her time came and the darkskinned gardener was on night duty and he was directed by the keeper to check on the chimps in the night-house periodically. Jumba was chained in one corner and Urakayee was tethered opposite him and she labored through the night, Ali told me, and the darkskinned gardener directed to do so checked on her occasionally (she was so very loud, he told Ali, I never knew an animal could make such wretched barbarous animal noises). In the morning, the keeper goes in and Jumba is bleeding at the neck because he'd been pulling on his chain during the night and it leaving its iniquitous circumference around his neck and the other monkey is lying on her side and the babe is halfway out of her. Urakayee is quiet by the time the keeper arrives (after his breakfast and cigarette) and Jumba is quiet; Urakayee appears tired and listless to the keeper and he enters the cage to get the baby ('I was going to pull it out,' he told Ali) and when he opens the cage door Jumba jumps up (to the extent he is able with his circular chaffe) and begins his howling, hooting, baring his canines and wretched barbarous noises fill the night-house and the place erupts with his hoots shakes the blood loose and the chains rumble and Jumba makes this hoot-ruckus and his blood runs thicker down his torso and (the keeper throws the empty tins at him marks him with his rifle) Urakayee doesn't move and the keeper approaches slowly (having lowered his gun and knows that a chimp is five times as strong as any man, even a female chimp, and that caution is always advised because they wily unpredictable African beasts and even though he carries a rifle and syringe of) upon closer inspection realizes that it is not emerging from Urakayee, that she lies partially on top of the angelic baby animal (the chimps beautiful when they are born pink-faced and brown eyed and undemoniac, he thinks: it's the darkskinned animals that are) and he can see the babe's head and right shoulder (thus having given the impression that he was still being birthed)— it appears as if she were attempting to push it back inside her body rather than expel him and he's dead, he tells Ali later: she killed him after she birthed him. But this keeper unnerved by the pushed back in monkey, by its broken neck and the look of calm sleep on the pink face and because of the baby hand pushed back in and the one shoulder almost in her chimpy sex and she couldn't do it, the keeper told Ali; Ali tells me later when he tells the story: 'We named him Vahé in your honor. A good Armenian monkey!' and we laughed about it for weeks afterward on the sabbath visits that I'd been making regularly (Juliana's where are you going? become regular also) and I think: *how to dispose of the barbaric flesh?* But I do not ask it of Ali or the keeper or even the darkskinned gardener from the south.

XI

AUGUST 1924 we are in the Cinema Rivoli. The seats are large and red, they are comfortable and the cinema is nice. I wear a new pair of shoes and although they are a size too big they look handsome on my feet; it is warm and the fans are running and they make noise. Now it is dark and there is a man in front of me and he is in the African jungle. The jungle is a nice place and he has animals to help him because he is alone: he is happy alone and with the animals and he doesn't speak. Nobody talks but they are running and swinging and the fans are still running overhead and so the fans make noise and he doesn't. This is my first time in the cinema. I am good and quiet. The other boys, the older boys, are loud and stupid when Hayrig is not looking. I am looking at the man and he is running and swinging on the branches. My feet do not hurt, I am sitting in the comfortable red velvet seats. I am resting arms on the armrests. Levon hits my arm off. I move my arm off because I am quiet and I am good and I am watching the moving pictures. They are moving; the man is running with the elephants and the monkeys. He is a strong man. He has a monkey friend; they are friends and he is not lonely. Then he is fighting someone and fighting for a long time and then a lion and then the lights are lighted and the fans running and we are all sad to stand up. We leave the cinema. This is my first time in the cinema. There is a poster outside the building and the man sits on top of a lion with his knife raised in the air above the name of the moving picture *The Adventures of Tarzan*. I like the moving pictures and the man and animals inside them. We are all sad now to go back to the Nest.

XII

I HAVE NOT wanted more than a small life and although a small man I am not entirely too insouciant, unformed or unclanned to know that some men's lives are not small and more true and the travels and the have-done and the have-acquired bigger, but I would have been, I have been contented with my small pleasures and small wonders: the flat in Ras Beirut, Rue Makdissi 4e B; polished brown loafers; coffees; the sweeties; a long mezzé; the cinema on Sunday afternoons; Corniche walks; and, of course, the sea out of view or viewing it, the wind, the sunlight; and unadorned a woman's teat, her legs, her sex, the lips fat, ruddy and open for me. I went the first when I was sixteen and it the first time I had my own money in my pocket and Émile took me there, downtown, he said, behind the Banque Suisse, near the Cinema Rivoli. I knew it, of course, but I'd not had the money in my pocket until that day, my first week's pay at Gembali's shop and we went after work that Friday evening, the muezzins could be heard then, or I thought I heard it, we climbed into a service and

Place des Martyrs, he said, and we got down there by the statue and up Rue de Damas and behind Rue Nahr Ibrahim. The stairway was dark and pissy on the first two floors and when we arrived at the place it was bare except for three chairs and we sat until an old painted woman entered and held up three fingers and took our money (not speaking the three lira exchange hands) and ushered us into another room with five chairs and two of them empty and sitting upon the other three three women, all of them middle-aged (*like the me I am now,* thinks) and old and Émile pointed at the one and I, following his lead, pointed at another, not looking at her, lift my arm and moving my index finger the requisite two centimeters to indicate the her to the left and one of them got up and took my arm (she was smiling and) led me to another room divided by a curtain (torn and dirtywhite) and I remember I could hear Émile on the other side of the curtain, but not his girl, his noises, and I didn't look at mine, I cannot say what she looked of, but I was aroused and wanted to see her cunt and she lay back on the bed and flipped up her skirt and she wore no knickers and I undid my trousers and I was aroused and although uncertain I lay on top of her and she knowing (but me not looking to see this knowing-look) took the penis of an adolescent boy and put it inside her cunt. She said, 'It's the first, eh?' And it was glorious as the moment of fucking it always is for this boy— and better than glorious with that whore and to be held in it and it hot inside her flesh and in that moment, the high moment of fuck it fuck it and I am as happy as I will ever be and the world is right and I want it always, to be doing it, she is hot inside her cunt and holds me hot and to do it to do it I could do it every day and then there are days that I do, so much money spent on the whores that I can only ever take the cheap ones behind Rue Nahr Ibrahim, not the nice ones that later it would be better to take; later on Émile only went to see those girls and chided me, the cheap whiskey, the cheap whore, but I don't mind, I love the Ritas any way I can get them: cheap and expensive and the tramway operator's wife, open your legs, darling, and I'll put it in. And she says not so fast darling, slow down my boy, and she is happy to make the man of me, she says, happy to provide this service, but I cannot do it cannot slow it and I'm looking at the dirtywhite curtain and then I can see the curtain because while we are doing it I didn't see only felt this warm held, something bigger than myself, and it's done and then I can hear Émile again behind the cloth and he is making noise, animal noises, and I want it again immediately but the whore gets up and leaves the room, 'You Armenians are fast,' she chides me, 'like hot metal.' Perhaps it is still and always me there, sitting on that mattress, it is uncovered, stained, threadbare and almost pitiful in its threadbareness; my trousers are around my ankles and I wear my shoes and my shirt is buttoned up. I would like for that woman to return to me and I would like to do it again but I have no more money today; but I cannot rise from the bed or lift my trousers or wipe my penis clean with my shirttails. I hold my penis and it is wet and all that day and the next I don't wash my hand to smell it and her again and again and the dream of her (think I could love) I want to take her out of that place and to fuck every day and she was beautiful, and when I return the following week I look for her but I cannot find her and the queue outside the bordello snakes around to the cinema, rows of men who wait with their hands in their pockets, who piss in corners when they're done and I take another Rita and then another the following week until I am months and years away from that first whore and all of the whores between us but it is not like that again, and I search for it in every whorecunt: that beautiful lovely warm and held. I want it every day even still.

XIII

I GUARDED THE ITEMS of my possession (that possession a
state of unease) inside the wooden box and the bit of twine and
the knucklebones and found marble (blue and white) were not
unusual and I carried my box from here to there in the yard to the
dormitory to the meal hall because otherwise the items in my box
appropriated by rascal and informant and self-promoter alike and
so we all of us bore our insecure goods in boxes and rucksack
from here to there—and classroom and of course I had my pencil nub, at one instance I had six of them (and were traded for the
blue and white marble, five for the one small globe which I didn't
shoot to preserve it better)—as if we were some bedouin camels,
thirsty and fatigued and yet unable to remove our property loads
because in their case to be beaten and in ours to be dispossessed.
The lot of my worldly goods was in constant flux here, attributa-
ble to the season and the needs and the boy whose auntie came for
him (leaving: 3 pencil nubs, 6 knucklebones, twines, a wooden
spoon, and bent screw) for the boy who could get it, or rather,

rush out the other boys who gathered around his bedding that night before he was scheduled to leave this place, and in this place our boxes and rucksacks sewn from rice bags were the two hundred-fifty-hectare estate of the Beka'a grape growers. as important and our vast holdings contained in our boxes: everything and more valuable here than blood and wine and so never left unattended and so always tried for and sought after by the others and the bigger and *Now, give it over* the arm torn of its socket and the split cheeks, etc.

The picture of the boy atop the elephant is nice. The boy is happy and he smiles, his hair is bright like a film star and his teeth are big white and he seems to kick the elephant forward with his legs and will. The elephant beneath the boy's loins is large and gray with his tusk upturned now as if seeking the peanuts and he is dancing a little bit and covered on his back by a large and lovely red and yellow drape and his forehead also covered in red (silk, yes) the same drapery and the boy sitting in a chair (yes) and bouncing on the elephant's back as they walk out of the picture toward infinity and happiness. The picture is torn at the edges and an elephant foot missing too, so three legs walk to the edge of the world (the image) outside to happiness and because the boy's family is far away the elephant is taking him there and hiding beneath the chair (you can't see it) they've got some good sweets for their journey overland through the desert (Der-el-Zor and) and across the high rivers (Euphrates and) and over the high mountains (Ararat and) to get to his family (his mother and) who await him with their arms outstretched and some of the arms filled with the things he would like to have: a pocketful of bright marbles; a wooden train set; black shiny boots, 10 pair; piles of sweeties; a monkey. He needs a house to put all of his things in and a big metal lock as big as ten hands to lock up his house with his things and his family inside; lock the house from the inside and the outside—ten biggest locks to do it; the elephant (Raja) can sleep outside in the *shed* (*build a big shed for Raja*) and after everything is locked up and all of the sweeties eaten up then kiss everyone hello! and the kisses of reunion and telling the stories of that horrible (now forgotten) time before when he carried his box from here to there *because he lost his small lock and so he had to do it to safeguard his*: 'we love you! we love you!' they shout and there are hundreds of the relatives who come and visit him at his house and they are all called   because we all have the same name here! And so guards this picture with life and limb, folded tightly into four at the bottom right of the insecure box.

XIV

These are the items in my box (10):
1. one half meter of twine, very strong; brown
2. the wooden spoon
3. 1 marble, cracked
4. 4 knucklebones
5. 2 walnuts (for trade), desiccated
6. smooth pebbles: 4
7. a steel spring
8. 1 yellow (cracked) button without the button-hole
9. 2 pencil nubs, smaller than my thumb
10. 2 fancy pictures from a magazine: a tall elephant; a nice lady

XV

—Was it terrible? Were you very lonely?

He knows how to respond because he knows without knowing it that speech is prescribed by unseeable specious speech-markers: by capital and clan and Juliana's love stories inside her head and the clan stories inside their heads and all of it before him: by decorum and its hefty accretionary stand: only possible to say (thinks: *To remember that place is first to remember the smells: the wretched latrines doorless whose odors permeated our shirts and torn pants; the watery soups filled with unknown and formless decayed matter; the unclean hands and faces and long bodies—the scent of dried urine and secreted perspiration and longing in the flesh, putrid. And after the smells the millenary dark days of winter when the hands and feet never warmed over for all of the months of the season and the hands tucked between the thighs at night to warm them and by morning warmed only to be made cold again by the day and elements; and empty bellies and the canings and the dark look of the Mairig, her scowl always heavy over us; her: You are a bad lot and You'll pay for it and Shut it or you'll pay for it; and the hollowed grieving bones which noisy and broken and clamoring again and again for the un-filled organs—the starved and appropriated machinery wanting meat and grain and sugary sweets above all living things: above tender-ness. The hatred that filled our unfilled organs but in sooth still that terrible fleshy organ clamor like one hundred bells for one tender (or at the least unhateful) word from that avatar, the one afternoon when she said, 'You've done well on your examination, boy,' and he, this cold-handed -footed -hearted boy who thought everything in him was saturated by the hate of her and not wanting anything else from this beastly god except two cups of fatty hot soup and he the saturated-hate boy smiled and bowed like the good trained circus boy and 'Thank you, Mairig' and he happy all day and the next (and hungry hungry) and this—this—the worst to bear, the most shameful. But something like:)*—No. I hardly remember a thing.

—. . . Do you, that is, do you: did you ever try to find anyone in your family?

—No, it's not possible in my case.

—I am sorry.

(a dog or trained ape aping the good boy routine for that kind tender word—for years he is the monkeyboy and mostly kicked and caned and evilly exhorted: Stupid feckless boy—and he saying: it is for two cups of fatty soup or an extra ration of bread, and he no different from every other one of them in that place—the hate-filled organs, the spewed killing stories of what they said (to each other at night in the barracks) how they would do it—strip her limbs and hair from her body, make her suffer and then she before them, cane highest, and

*they thanking and scraping, bowing and aping the good circus mon-
key, good dogs: kick me.*)—Nothing to be sorry for. And you,
where did you study?

—At the Hripsime Secondary School for Girls. And the nuns
were cruel teachers.

—You work at the Office of Education?

—Yes, I'm a stenographer and typist.

—Your father works there also?

—No, no. My father's been dead these many years, a
Kharphertsi, he died from meningitis when I was a girl. It's
just me, my younger brother, and my mum: she's also from
Kharphert. You don't

—No. Not where they're from or who they were.

—I'm sorry.

—Yes. (*Because in sooth, we tried everything to get it: hard
study, low bows, stretched smiles, tucked arms, shirts, running fast—
and none of it worked in a predictable manner. On the one day the one
boy her favored, and he two cups of that special fatty soup and we
looking on and the next the same boy lying low because he now out of
favor for the handsome football runner or the first place in the second
class and this he now eating the fatty soup and thick crusted bread
(and a sweetie later?). She the unpredictable and vicious, our vicari-
ous god teaching us that the flesh is feckless because even hungry it
yearns for the god's smile; even hate-filled it empties the organs like
airless balloons for her pleasure, unpredictable smiling pleasure—
and for this smile we all of us the chained shamed monkeyboy—held
in check by our flesh and its unnourished needs.*) Perhaps they also
Kharphertsi, we arrived from there in '22.

—Then it must be so. Let's say it's so. I'll tell my mother: a nice boy from the town of Kharphert. She'll be happy.

—Yes.

—She used to help at an orphanage in Aleppo, before I was born. She'll like you. She washed there, I think, before she got the job with the Demirdjian family; before she met my father. This is my favorite by Adamo, 'Tombe la neige, tout est blanc de désespoir.'

(and does not think; he is: *Your parents also without their clan or their parents and the attenuated blood flows in you, stretched out across the Der-el-Zor and the Lebanon because we all of us here adrift and because the past is always unspoken heavy and ever-present like some invisible unfurled ribbon and we entangled in it as we are in our own blood; like the unfeathered and unflying beastly bird pushing trapped in my breast;* thinks: *She is not beautiful—small of stature and wide of hip, the nose, mouth—nothing to marvel at or notice even: not thin, not fat; brown hair brown eyes. And yet I am undone. By the eyes and yet not the eye itself: by the dark hollows beneath them. She a girl of twenty-two. She is young and she wears black shadows beneath her eyes like some women wear rouge and lipstick, and she doesn't cover this darkness (yet) and I never told her in all of these many years how I hated it when she began to cover up this beautiful darkness—this preeminent and permanent black specter, that it made the thirtyish man think he could love her then, want to love her and be better than the man he was because he loved imperfection, he loved the boldness of the irreversible sad nightmark on her face: a bold truth in the mendacious decorous world with its unsaid unsayable things. And over the years she covered it up and he lost this thought of her, he lost her darkness, her difference, and she farther away now and he unable to see back, to find his way back to the twenty-two-year-old girl with a black belt beneath her eyes like dark sunlight.*) —Juliana, will you be my girlfriend?

—Yes yes yes.

—Shall we go to the cinema?

—Is it the hour already? Have you seen his others? I have loved every film with Cary Grant in it.

XVI

Mama could not arrive today: because:

1. attends mass
2. she is tied to a post and crying
3. and she cannot escape (wants to)
4. she cannot walk she lost her feet in the desert
5. she is lost (in the desert) and crying
6. and she cannot escape (wants to)
7. a man holds her hostage he wants money
8. she doesn't have any money: washes rich people's (like the Sunday samaritans and Hamra ladies) clothes
9. she is lost
10. in another place and she cannot speak the (dead) language

Tomorrow she arrives (at the front gates): because:

1. no mass tomorrow
2. she breaks the chains on her bedpost and
3. runs away (fast) to here

4. she sits atop a mule (or elephant) and
5. rides her elephant (Raja) here to the front gates
6. she kills that man
7. kills the Sunday samaritans and gets all their money from a chest
8. she arrives at the front gate atop Raja
9. says, 'Bonjour mon petit!'
10. 'Bonjour Maman!': we kiss and hug (we go to another place together atop Raja)

XVII

BECAUSE IT HAS BEEN FOR LOVE. And my life unhistoried (by the unsigned cabinets; an unseeing servant girl; the long southwesterlies in winter unquitted unchanged by my perambulatory form or the raised arm; the slanted light terribly unobstructed made the girl's cotton into fleshy halo, purveyor to hallowed flesh) and so I made histories unmade them in my head and placed them next to thoughts and memory and notmemory made so because these are the things in a man's life made so and because I was always a boy not to have lived I lived it and because I was always silent I spoke out loudly where only you could hear me (you unable to listen except here in the interior fleshiness among the turgid heaving organs) and I thus considered it a betrayal: mine own death and twenty-two years from now when I will finally be relieved (yes to die and to be killed) I will think just before death that a bold suicide would have been something: returning to the sea and the quiet eternal warmth, the touch of water complete and there I am myself and quiet and there with all of skin touched as if held tightly and yes the longing to return to the place that is unreturnable, but I never did it, not once (a half-tried once which is not a once) because: if all of the histories are dead and all of it is scattered about the earth (the blood of it) then at the very least I can say: for love. I carried on in the darkest days with my woods and the bodies of girls because in the sweet lazy canvas of your imagined body I wanted to make what you gave me not in vain and somehow a small victory, an unhistoried vanquish, made so by the blood's continued rush through veins and artery into out of a pumping heart to remember you and so I am sorry, dear Mother, not to have made for you the progeny, not to leave on the land (the dispersed and attenuated blood) some— boy digging the soil or some—girl, a virgin, willing to bear and bear the rest of the clan down through into History, thicken the blood and bring it home and gather it together and saying 'We are here!' and by this she means we can return, we can remake the unremembered the unhistoried because the progeny can do it, our durance at its end, we all of us break the wind with our bodies put the light off its course with enough of our forms—so why didn't he do it? this your boy who was not your boy? Because (turgid and indolent): he would have (*I would have*) slaughtered mine own progeny like a sow eats her young, like the mythic goddess ate hers, like any dead mother; I cannot bear it: the wars; the bloodletting; the untold things. I cannot.

Because I am not from this place. Because there is distance and it is a wide gap made by land and unwilled journey and also by the tongue itself because of: what it cannot say, what it no longer knows how to say, what it does not know—the language makes me dead, I speak dead words and then I'm seeking a body via these (now dead) words: Նորից զարուն եկավ, զարուն աննրման do you hear it? I'm singing it for you always and again, not the French love song that I sang for the girl, I loved her here, she also not from this place: is it this which creates the sadness because I have always been out of place—my body and my tongue, the one body and the myriad tongues; I don't remember: the Armenian (before it was dead); the Turkish (it beaten from the meat like one beats the horrific lamb); the Armenian taught back to me at the Nest, beaten back word by word (the rod blows) makes the tongue anew (What is your Christian name?); the Arabic to buy food and welcome and a coffee and a shawarma sandwich please and drinks and whores and cigarettes and Ali and; the French for the Christian ladies, their questions about this smooth edge, the merci madames and pas de problèmes and the tourists from Europe and America bundled into our city.

Because I can never get it back.

Because I am not from this place.

Because: the untraversible distance of death death itself cannot traverse. A perambulator who can never arrive nor ever return. There is not Heaven nor Hell, nor New Jerusalem round the bend of the mountain and this untraversable distance for the man distanced from land and language is the last and most painful and the least livable with because death itself cannot abet it: I can never get you back, Mother, not in all of the flesh of this world (newly created or no), nor in the spectered notflesh; not even upon my own death. And this, this ultimate betrayal of myth and God Himself I cannot bear and of course there is only the bearing of it: to do it to do it for as long as I shall live and for as long as I shall not live—earthworms, garbage, dust of the manly flesh.

Still, there has been my soft and slight the limps and sad madonna girl: the afternoon sunlighted discovery of the cotton-sheathed teat—revealed to me and then love and it is this last and long and unrequitable organ energy: this love: that has made it worth the bearing, made it livable and this girl who did: who brought joy and a certain sunlighted happiness into that afternoon boudoir. Forget about the progeny because in that moment of grace, the light and beauty of Béatrice, the forbidden fruit on earth and Jumba had his Urakayee and I my own Béatrice. And it is enough now. The organs may cease, the blood spill itself onto the concrete and the boys play in its red-thick flow. And who will needs desire traverse the distance of mine own death? And who pass a lifetime with such an unrequitable and horrible demoniac bone desire as to make the desirer into idiot, unspeaking unhistoried fool? None I hope. Now for this brief interlude, the French music plays and rolls off of the balcony in waves: I can see the sea from where I lie and with it am contented because of love. And when they come for me I will be ready: tomorrow or twenty-two years from now when this place erupts again with the chimes of war and hubris and long embattled blood and clan and capital and one confession pitted against the other: come do it; kill it. It is natural to do it. And then we'll forget it again, unhistory it for you before after death.

XVIII

thinks: *war is my god, our Father—he made us makes us who we are*

XIX

—My god you look old *smiles and nods*.

—Me? and your paunch like some brooding deepsea fish there—a middle-aged brood fish *and they kiss on each cheek, the hearty slap to the back*.

—Yes *looks down at his belly* perhaps too many sweetmeats, eh friend—

—Still in the wood shop?

—Of course. You? You've got your shop? And how are your boys?

—Yes the shop is fine, business is good! I've got three now: the one in Ashrafiyeh, the one in Ras Beirut and the other here downtown and the wife is fine and busy spending my money! and I'm sure anytime soon those boys will be a hand taller than me. The oldest is at the Jesuit secondary, wants to be a doctor, and the others think only of football and comic books! But your wife?

—She's well. We've only just returned from Ba'albeck, we saw Om Koulsoum perform—have you been this summer?

—No, no, we're off to France for a few weeks to see my wife's family. Take the boys to Paris and the South to the beaches and then of course they're up in Aley since June while I sweat it out down here during the week, too lazy to drive up the mountain on some days.

—Shall we get another bottle? *he pours* It's been too hot, no?

—Yes and yes, are you in the mountains this summer?

—No, just for day trips. We're here mostly.

—My God man, it's been a long time, hasn't it? And then to see you on the street like this on such a hot day— how long has it been? Five years?

—Yes I should think, last time I saw you was in Hamra.

—Right, it was just after my third boy was born. And we talked about how that idiot died; thank God he made it to our Bird's Nest, no?

—Yes *he pours*.

—Because without him they had it out for you, didn't they, those boys they just couldn't bear to have you with us— you thrown onto the train like some extra piece of luggage and I remember it well: we all thrown together in those hot boxcars and I swore to myself then that I would never be made to travel like some beast again, all stuffed in and it hot and nothing to drink and for weeks until we arrived here and you in a corner and those boys around you and you probably unable to understand any of it, *he pours* right? I have wondered about it, the things we could not ask when we were boys—about how you came to be dropped off at the orphanage in Kharphert; how you spoke not one word of Armenian and your unintelligible cry for months that we couldn't understand until you slowly began to understand us and the boys wanting to beat that Turkish out of you like one might beat a pet dog for disobeying and shitting the carpet and you there shat upon and pissed by the boys in those hot boxcars and I never knew and wanted to know: how did they know you were one of us *he pours* those missionary fellows? I mean, where did they find the trace of it? Because you even looked like them when you arrived with your pants and headdress and the boys couldn't stand it very well, especially the bigger boys who remembered clearly what had happened to their parents and uncles and aunties in 1915, and I mean you looked like them and spoke like them and they couldn't bear it, couldn't bear one more humiliation the hatred so strong in those boys and me not as old, probably eight at the time, and not as hating, no, not as remembering either, perhaps and of course I knew my mother would come get me when she could, she working for that rich family in Ashrafiyeh and so and the other thing I wanted to know is how then did you ever get it back, I mean, they—

—— *he pours* Pardon?

—Today man, I'll tell you the truth: it shames me what they did. And you never made them sorry for it or brought the moral rod out later to show them it and how wrong it was and even though Hayrig told us that we should not hate you or the others like you you can perhaps understand now, as a man, and now that we can speak of these things honestly forthright speciously that it was perhaps our duty to do it—that it must needs be beaten from you, that vile black mark of Cain, that Turk mark, like one marks his dog for ownership by his rod and sly kicks—it was in fact our duty: do you see that now? Our desire and implacable duty to get you back from your experience as his dog? To make you back

into one of us. Repercussed, see? It was for your good and *he*
pours there is no shame about it, no not at all, for what we did, because you see it had to be done given what they'd done to us: it
was us or them in the end and so sacrifices had to be made. Repercussed, see? I always wanted to ask you, though, you always
seemed at peace, you quiet at the least but to ask: did you ever
hate us for it? Did you *pours pours pours* I mean thank God for the
idiot arriving with his ugliness like some horrible dress, my God
and God forgive me: but he was horrid, wasn't he? He shined
shoes on Hamra in the years afterward, shined my own boots and
Italian leathers, and he got killed that way I mean some people
say suicide because he'd have seen the truck and I think he did it
on purpose: just walked out into the oncoming traffic like some
unholy djinn to meet the Maker and so no way that he could ever
be in Paradise no, eh?, no no no way at all, poor bastard, but did
you: I mean did you hate us for it?

—*no no no* Pardon? Pardon? Pardon?

XX

AND HE A MAN who does not read books and no more curious or piqued by them than any beast may be and thinks: *I could take a walk along the Corniche* because he only ever reads the dailies the weeklies and the scant journal that has come in the post and this because of the requisite habits of living and next day's weather and the football scored up and so in the apartment there are few of them: the leather-bound bedside Gospel and some others Juliana has purchased because she passed a bookshop and thinks she ought to have some like she ought to have an automatic clothes washer and an embossed lizard handbag from France and then buys the new (foreign) book the bookseller tells her she ought to purchase and returns home with her purchases: the foreign handbag and the foreign book and next day wears the handbag and the book lies on a side table and next to the cut flowers and so he doesn't think *Perhaps there is something in one* or that he will open the Gospel because he needs something and *Maybe it's in there because I don't see it anywhere else and I've looked* and perhaps it's always been in there and walks to the bedroom and not thinking picks up one of Juliana's purchases on the way and reads: *You cant know yet. You cannot know yet whether what you see is what you are looking at or what you are believing. Wait. Wait.* And strange, thinks, because he hadn't thought about it, that he's

found something inside and it findable in a book, and he thinks
that he will wait now: for Juliana who will be home later who is
less and less contented because he (more and more) unsure and
seeing that boy everywhere and beginning his walks on the sabbath and so is not at mass as he once was but (like a savage, she
says) gone off to that place with the wild animals and he can't
yet say to her what it is, something, because he himself does not
know; and he thinks that if he just keeps on, the perambulator, he
will know and when he does it will be all right: the boy, the animal, himself now. And strange that a book has told him so and he
a man who does not abide books, not reads, he the perambulator
peripatetic wood slayer smoother cutter and cinema-goer and does
not read and then on the one afternoon in the fall of 1963 walking around the apartment and lies on his back and hands beneath
his head and smokes and smokes and gets up and thinking *How
will I do it? There must be something?* and unlike the not reader
walks toward the bedroom in search of the Gospel and picks up
the discarded purchase and opens it and it is true: wait: wait: and
so he will do it; he waiting and walking on the sabbath and Juliana saying 'I can't take it anymore' and he the walker and the
waiter to see when he can see it differently—the way it must
needs be seen; something; to see a true story so that he will know
and when he knows it he will rest easy and Juliana will love him
easy and all is well; wait—wait, he'll do it. Puts the book down,
discarded now and returns to the balcony hears the car horns
blaring below and looks out into the distance and that something
inside the man like the trapped bones of his own body, like such
an awesome and tumultuous unfeathered and unflying bird pushing its wings against his chest, pushing down there and the pres-

sure builds and the unflying bird pushes against his chest muscles and not pushing out but into his organs and creates there the heaviness, the need for something he cannot name, pushes the not reader to look even in the ascetic desiccated unelectrified fleshless place for it (but that is the only time he does it) and finds there the wait wait and he will. He looks at the sea now, the monster still inside the hollowed grieving bones and thinks: unbeknownst to me. I am a man and it is unbeknownst to me. And thinks as he has always thought, how it is better to seek it in the flesh and he continues seeking it this way, as he has always done behind the Banque Suisse, near the Cinema Rivoli, and Rita comes to visit him at the shop and he thinks to discard this wait wait and forgets about the ways of seeing and looking. Thinks: in the flesh I'll find it and later, months later, in March, he does it in Yusef's salon: a certain slant of light during the afternoon soirée and there it is before him: her white linen become translucent by the light streaming in through the west-facing windows. And for a quarter of an hour he is transfixed by the servant girl bending and serving the drinks, she unaware of the transformative light, she the unnoticeable and unseen girl until the four o'clock sun streams in unfettered by the pulled-up blinds and transforms cotton into fleshy halo, hallows flesh—the girl becomes a beauty, Béatrice, angelic he would say if he believed it, by the afternoon light until the Madame Yusef notices the transformation or she thinks it too hot too bright the sunlight in her husband's eye and drops the blind suddenly and the girl returns to opaque, the fabric its old coarse washed-out cotton, the disappeared madonna, and he remembers it: seek it in the flesh and he won't wait now. He will act, he thinks. He will act.

XXI

I WOULD ADD THAT I wanted to be good, that I could have
been better than I was because of this want; that until ten or
eleven I intended to be good, although even then I understood
that what I wanted and what was were as different as the sweetie
is from the fatty dinner soup. Because although I never questioned: heaven hell and the natural hierarchies and virtues of the
strong and athletic and bigger boys and masters, I still could not
do it, could not love Him and could not understand, although yes
accept—as the child will accept all of the contradictory nonsense
of his keepers: the contradictions: if He were good and to be
loved and feared and if His power bigger than anything else,
then: the horrid place, the horrid people, the Mairig, the long
cold days and long hot canings and the hungry and bigger boys
and the eternal out of place, the unclanned boy?—His plan. Until eleven believing (the contradictory nonsense of his keepers)
that there was a plan, like a teacher lays out the mathematical
problem for the hungry cold caned boys: 'Ratiocination, boys!'
Mr Hovannes says, writing his numbers for them. 'Add it up
quickly!': there is a plan and (accepting all of the contradictory
nonsense of his keepers) it would be true and good—as I could
be if it were possible and then in early adolescence understand-

ing: it was not possible to be good, never the coincidence for this boy; perhaps for the Big Garo's and Bedros' and well-tailored Andranik with his three shops and three boys (and a mother cleaning houses until she could get him out of the Nest)—but not for this one. Because for the weak unvalorous and demoniac unclanned boys—the boys that could have been better than they were, but too filled: first with hate envy and later lust sacrilege—the good and the possible would never coincide. And so I never did it, not once, a half-tried once which is not a once, like this:

It is hot and we are at the public beach near Raouche on the west side (because unpaid today and out of funds for the paying beach) and so we here with all of the poor, the riffraff, Juliana says: the ragged Palestinian camp hordes and their screaming running boys and the southern village Shi'ia with their running screaming boys and this the last time she will ever come to the public beach and she is lying on her towel, reading a foreign book, her black-rimmed sunglasses on her face and a white bathing suit (she will not bathe). I am in the sea on my back and rolling with the waves and the camp boys and the village boys are loud and running and I am moving with the waves and staring up at the blue sky that becomes white as I stare and the heat of the day moves skyward.

The water holds me loosely and yet it is a ubiquitous loose, tight around the seams of my skin. I see the white sky, hear the screams of the boys (they're happy and running happy), and Juliana reads or pretends to read: ignoring the mothers and other women; and I think: *I am contented like this*. Held and warm and the sea always warm and however sad she is: constant. And then I am swimming beneath the water and farther out to sea: pushing with my legs and pulling with my arms because I am happy for the happy camp village boys but I would like quiet now, the ubiquitous loose hold and quiet beneath the water and so I push-pull the water with my legs and arms and my lungs begin to feel like millstones pulling me forward and out into the quiet and deep so that it is cooler and quieter and all around me happiness: my eyes are open and I see sea as if seeing for the first time my rushing blood, heavy organs, millstone lungs. And now it is as if the millstone is round my neck and like a blessing, a chain, pulling me on faster and faster and deeper into the dark salt warm sad Mediterranean. And for one moment I am the believer. I believe in Him, in plans, in ratiocination: in meaning and Paradise, the New Jerusalem appears before my eyes as we make the descent down the mountain; in Love. *Ah, Juliana* I think (or *Vosto* or *Jumba* dependent on the time of this once—was it five years ago or last year on my birthday? or two months ago when Jumba died?) and it all falls apart, breaks apart like the millstone explodes from my chest, from round my neck and it pushes me up until I can see green then blue then light and hear a horrible animal sound and the boys again—a distant tinny pitched sound from the shore— and the animal sounds, I realize, are mine because this the animal pushed back to his original form: the beast who wrenched the millstone from his neck and pulled himself to the surface of the sea because the beast must breathe, because the animal must live: more than God, more than Love, more than the ratiocinated idea of Paradise which, he remembers, is a lie. And this is his once which is no once; Juliana screaming from the shore: 'Why do you have to do that?' and he waving back to her: not happy but not unhappy either.

XXII

THAT MONKEY HATED ME. And I knew it for more than thirty years and for more than thirty carried the image of him: the dark eyes and pink-brown face and then black and wrinkled and grayed and still hating, his front teeth removed ten years ago, and he always still in that place while I swam in the sea, took my coffees and fucked the Ritas, and lived—that monkey ape primate Pongidae Pan troglodyte Jumba lived in his four-by-two-meter box.

And were Jumba and I to encounter each other in the street he could pull out each of my limbs with one adventurous tearing; torn the arm arm leg leg then tossed the stub torso a long city block. Yet I had no more fear of Jumba than a city man fears the wharfside felines who've piled up their species into a posse, a battery of annoyances and dung-makers and loud latenight at the bordello makers, and bear diseases and when they accumulate too readily, they tossed off with a shotgun or poison meat or into the sea and drowned. The man-beast, the 'little man' as the Africans call him, so little feared, so entirely within our control that the city boy can love him like him dress him up and take him to dinner and laugh at his antics, his inability to eat correctly, his poor speech, make him wear a child's dress and a hair ribbon and too small shoes and paint his face and *will make you laugh see the monkey, he's a monkey and he loves it here, he loves to see you see him laugh he will make you happy he is happy the jungle is far away.* He is a terribly stupid beast, he can no longer inspire the wild legends, the Tarzan swings branch to branch in the tree and his beastly friend Cheetah is dead and not even the tamest myth because we have made you our childish amusement and conquered your race and erased you caged you and hidden you away because every week I visit you here and you are still here sitting shitting throw the feces through the steel bars and crouched in your corner and pucker your lips again and again as if you are happy; you look happy to the children. And the children love you, they come once a year with their parent grandmother grandfather an uncle the neighbor and you exist when they see you (for a handful of minutes) until the lion's cage the elephant corner and you are not a caged stupid unmoving shitting caged— because you are like a picture show and you are bright and disappeared and the lights come up (the fans run above our heads if it is hot in the summertime) and then disappeared. Unexisted until next year, the following year's visit to the zoological gardens when we'll take a photograph because on s'amuse. On profite. O to be well and truly entertained!

XXIII

WE ARE OUTSIDE and seated in rows on the warm concrete. We have new shirts and we are wearing shoes. We have been sitting in rows for more than one hour; I am uncomfortable and my feet are heavy and numb in my new shoes. The Mairig is walking up and down our rows; she carries her rod like a black bat between her fingers; it flies up, haphazard, a strange uneven arc, before it descends on the boy who does not sit up straight; 'Sit up,' she is saying to him. We sit in rows and the small boys are in the front rows and the bigger boys stand in the back. The cameraman is holding his hand up in the air; his camera is big and held upright by a tripod; I would like to know how a camera makes pictures. We are sitting for a long time. The mairigs stand next to us; Hayrig arrives and he stands in the front row; he is wearing a nice suit and tie. This is a photograph boys, he says to us, for our friends in America. Our friends in America would like to see you happy. *We are grateful for the help of America.* Our hair is combed and my shoes are nice; I have nice shoes on my feet.

After we have taken the picture we are allowed to play freely in the yard. We return our shoes and we put our old shirts back on. I would like to see this photograph but we cannot see it.

Weeks later, Hayrig tells us that the people in that place are happy with our photograph and he takes us to the cinema and I wear new shoes again. I am happy in the cinema.

XXIV

BECAUSE, JULIANA, you could never see me there. You see
the man lifts the coffee to his lips; hauls the bags of tinned milk,
rice and chicken; raises his glass for more whiskey, more ice,
more wine. The man who smells of tobacco and garlic in the
mornings; he picks his nose; his skin is dry, peels; he has few sym-
pathetic words for you; reads the daily, the weekly; fewer ca-
resses; he works and works. And you live with him for fourteen
years, cook for him, clean his shirts, the floors, arrange flowers in
a vase, buy a book for the bookcase, mold yourself tightly, you
do the good things, the cookclean things, a wife's domain and
yours is sharp, clean and organized. And you could not see his
thinks? could not see his *must needs?* and it is this shame. You said
nothing. You walked out and closed a door in our flat and we
didn't speak of it. We never did. But she is perpetually between
us, our silent banshee, she wails outside our windows.

Or it was like this, darling: I could not hold it, it came forth,
exploded outward and my thoughts and my unthoughts and the

things I didn't want or claim—the lot of it was coming forth, un-bidden: the boy Vosto, the fledgling ape corpse, the shy and limps servant girl, pushing out of me, unbidden and finally made me do it, to think it, and you are fixing coffee in the kitchen and I am on the balcony, it is a Sunday, and I sit on the swing and I am swing-ing, pushing up and back with my foot, and all of it returns in this moment: pushes forth as if the bird itself finally explodes free from my chest and it forces this act and I can't control its flight, the arc outward taking my tangled organs skyward and it flies sanguine forth and you come toward me with the small demitasse of Turkish coffee on a tray for me, sweetened as I prefer it, and in the same moment it explodes from my chest (you don't see it?) and the speaking Vahé says it to you as you give him his sweet coffee—I loved the girl.

—Yes?

And you don't believe me, there is no credence for it, cannot credit the man, your husband, who sits on the swing of the bal-cony in the early morning, sips his morning coffee, and from the ether, you think, from out of nothing, fabricates a story, a fan-tasy, 'A lie,' you say about loving a limps Arab servant girl? But this husband insists, he gets up from the balcony swing and he looks at you, sees you: the officious secretary arrived home early from work, she is tired and she looks tired, she is older, fatter, too conciliatory, he knows all of her places, he thinks, but it is not this that causes him to speak to her, finally, it is because he has real-ized that en fait he wants it told, wants a little bit of truth between them like a carpenter will use a little bit of oil on his oilstone, and that she is a good woman, a good Armenian wife, and he must give her something of himself finally, some truth of himself, because in all of their years together he has been the notlistens Vahé and today he will make something true, less of the lies, because, he thinks, *he does have this affection for her* and thinks this truth is correct and 'I have loved Yusef's domestic.'

You place my coffee on the small balcony table and you turn from me, return to the kitchen, you close the kitchen door and I could hear it shut-up from the balcony, its hinges loud and then shut. And we didn't speak of it, we never did. (You did not say: *You are not right. A Muslim girl: after what they did to us? If I could kill you I would do it. I can't bear it anymore. You must go. Now. Tonight at the latest. Do you listen? There's no going back this time. No reversal of fortune. I can't bear it anymore:—a Mohammedan girl?* because a wife must not? Or because you also did not know how to speak it?) At dinner that night I told a funny story about Mr Gembali and the boys and you listened and we turned off the lights and we undressed and we lay on our bed. I continued my walks to the zoologique on the sabbath and because Jumba had died the previous month (a heart attack, Ali told me), I took my pistachio nuts to the elephant corner; Raja loved the pistachio nuts I brought for her.

But I cannot be sure of this speaking—did I do it after fourteen years of notlistens, speaks only for the empty glass, the more coffees, the buy me a gâteau from Michel's? Because to speak such a thing entails a listening and listening the possibility of such a comprehension and you could never comprehend, darling—to love an indigent adolescent Palestinian maid?—Perhaps I could have said, Loved Yusef's wife (Maronite, dressed-up, made-up, officious and beautifully tailored on most days) and then perhaps you would have hated me, comprehended it, and we'd have continued apace—but not that other love, because to listen to such a thing is to understand that tomorrow we will rise from our beds as black crows and we will fly out our balcony doors and head northward then east and we'll return to those villages surrounding the rocky outcropping and mothers await us, fathers and uncles till fields with hands raised and openhanded to welcome us back. Our houses as we left them, our siblings play in the orchards. We'll make mulberry taffies we'll eat flat bread we'll slaughter a young lamb and cook its flesh. (And we'll never again eat grass for our dinner.) And we'll fly out of this place and when we arrive we will say: the seasons have turned on their head and time is illusory, take off your wristwatches, take off the sun calendar, and hold it hold it, we'll follow the moon's light: we are here and returned. And no more possible. Blood fantasy.

XXV

I WOULD HAVE SAID I fell in love with her form. Because: it was beautiful, she beautiful, and then I loved her. And it was not perchance the bruised arms or the look of her when I looked up, and this look like the small birthmark on my left arm: I cannot trace the beginning or end of knowing it, it always dark and part of me and when I finally looked at the girl I saw it there: the dark look, the dark marks on her forearms when she bent to serve the drinks and the long sleeves of her dress fell back and revealed them; the fear and sadness and out of place and wary like a street mongrel always there, already there, and then I saw it for the first time but I didn't love her then, not yet.

Did I see him doing it?

Making and remaking that look on her pointed and thinned face? Giving her the marks on her arms and the places she regularly hid from me: the back, the buttocks, her thighs. No and then yes; I see him doing it. She is in the kitchen and standing on her step stool, it is the last year of her step stool. And her father will arrive tomorrow from the south to collect her wages, perhaps she is happy that tomorrow she will see her blood kin, even though it is the stern father and even if he comes only for the wages and he doesn't bring her mother or any one of her sisters or small brother but perhaps some news of them, she thinks. Therefore she hums as she stands on the step stool and washes the lunch plates and platters, it is a popular love song and she has heard it on the girls' radio. He walks into the kitchen and she is startled because he seldom walks into the kitchen. She turns and she greets him with her sirs and masters and he says he would like some water now and she steps off of her stool and she is a small girl and goes to get his glass. She turns and hands it to him, she never looks in his face and so gives him the glass looking at the floor or his shined shoes and then she spills some of it because not looking she hits his raised arm and the glass falls to the floor and breaks and his shoes are wet and the hem of his pants and she is afraid now not because of the beatings he gives her, because he does beat her like one beats the street mongrel, she begins crying and she is afraid of this more than anything—her unstoppable cries that bring on his blows because he hates that she cries, loathes the small crying girl in his kitchen, and she doesn't want to do it, but it comes upon her like some strange and dark beast and will not leave her and so she is on the floor covering her head and neck and he is beating her with his fists and she is crying, thinks: Mama, I want to go home—this what she hates most— that he brings her again and again to this thinking place. Says: 'Please Monsieur, let me wipe your shoes'; thinks: *I want to go I won't eat too much; I'll haul the dung or build a trench; I'm a good girl.* Because she was his to do it. His girl brought up from Ein el-

Helweh. Her father, polite and darned coat and scuffed shoes at his door waiting for her wages, never walks through the apartment, doesn't see his eldest girl today, takes the money and merci-merci and his departure with his hands in his pocket. And: 'She is a good girl, sir?' And Yusef's yes, not looking at the girl's father—too busy or tired or impossible, because my darling, you and yours invisible hateful mongrel. We don't see you like we don't see the wall pipings or the corners in a room. Like we don't see the hands that shaped the bread we ate for breakfast or pounded the meat (we eat the meat, see the meat). This whiskey appears in my hand and I don't notice the hand that brought the glass or the ice or lifted the silver tray: do you notice the light, darling? Only if it is in your eyes and burns or hot, otherwise you see your visage in the mirror not the light that makes it, only the redness of your eyes from crying, they are swollen and your lip bleeds, you touch it, taste your blood, see the blood in your eye spreading out like oil on water. Like I never saw him beat you or your longing for your mama in the south and your sisters and brother and the kindly touch and the playfulness of evening with your cousins and the feast days and the gossips and walking through the camp barefoot and happy on the sunny afternoons with your cousins and sisters—I couldn't see it when I looked at you, when I looked up from the outstretched hand past the bruises and marks on your forearms to your chest, your visage— even then you were the mechanical monkey giving me my whiskeys, coffees, salted nuts in the afternoons from a silver tray. Nothing but a girl, a peasant camp girl, who lifted and proffered and never looked at us and silent like a good girl and stepping up and down from that stool and whether or not he fucked you I can't say, it is likely, the beatings the fuckings, but it is of no matter—what matters? Only this: I loved you like I loved the not-seen light, the sea, the high spring winds—what I couldn't see or seeing didn't know (salt warm sad). Did it matter if you and I were the same discarded unseen flesh? And out of place and would it have mattered, darling, if I'd told you or saved you or loved you in the flesh? Know this: I loved you in my mind and in my internal organs fleshy place I gave it all to you and I could have saved all of us—the three of us uncaged, unhanded, out and out and free. We could have tasted freedom together, didn't we do it? Didn't we do it?

XXVI

IF ONLY I'd been able to get it out. The unflying unfeathered and trapped inside flesh like the chest bones: the headless wretched bird indistinguishable from the bones of our flesh: we become the vogel and it us. We unflying stripped and deformed beasts and trapped inside those walls and seeing the sea in the distance but unable to go there and touch it or bathe except for that first time upon our arrival to this place and in the summer months as the Mairig decreed it. (I light another cigarette.) And we more contained than walls: by hunger and cold winter, dark rod beatings, and more than these: by aphorism, by the morality lessons, by the rumors in the dormitory, by fear and shame and what was not said (silent known imagined). How can something as fleeting and weightless or more so! more! than smoke have the power to make and unmake us? How can *thinks* tilt the seeing and ignoble the flesh and create pain as the hunger and cold and floggings did? Because this also true: when I arrived at the Nest I knew not one word of Armenian; I was a Turk boy: the vile, hated mongrel. I don't remember: knowing the enemy's tongue (or the original loss of mine own); the relearning of it in the Nest; being that vile hated animal. I remember Vosto arriving at our gates: the decimated fleshless boy, that horrible beast pushing out from his chest, his head sores and large nose and the look of him: disgrace and shame, the fucked-one; and I was happy because I knew in the looking that he would save me and I had prayed to God and when Vosto arrived I knew He had answered me and that I would get other things also: a trip with the samaritan, a wife someday, children, a house and nice shoes eventually. I remember Vosto's arrival. I remember the sea around the bend of the mountain; our bathing in the Mediterranean for the first time; his saving look; and the Mairig's twice-weekly Bible readings. She would sit in her chair and the hundreds of us at her feet and her cane at her feet in anticipation because sometimes the stories took us up out of that place: when the burning bush speaking not burns; and Moses doesn't look at it, listens; and Pharaoh is wildly horribly defeated and the sea throws up walls so that men may walk through them undrowned. But sometimes we sat there before her and uncomfortable and tired and hungry and wanting only to sleep awhile or without volition sleeping the while and if seen that hard cane descending upon our heads and Vosto says, 'Please Mairig, let me kiss your foot.' And she:

'Impious wretch—stupid beast' and rains her rod on his shoulders and he crouched at her feet kissing her feet the while, kissing the hem of her dress, then covering his head and please Mairig and then nothing but the sound of the beating (we the rest of us quiet and obedient); and to see his blood; and she stops only when Hayrig comes out of the far building and says to her to stop it and she angry with him stops it.

Or because I tried to keep my eyes from closing, and devised trick upon trick to do it: digging my fingers into the palm; pinching my legs; shaking my head slightly from one side to the other; biting my tongue, the inside of my cheek, my palm; and all of the boys tell me how stupid I am, that the clever ones sleep peacefully in the rear of the assembly and that if seated toward the front one must be more clever. I was not and flogged for it and deserving of it because to be stupid is to pay with blood and flesh. And I did it: (rains down the cane) 'Impious wretch—Turk-dog. A shame to your race: stupid dirty boy.' The boy crouches at her feet, kisses the booted foot and like Magdalene would wipe them if he could with his hair or flesh and presses the hem of her skirt to his mouth: 'Please Mother: I didn't. It was not me.'

'You are a stupid devilish boy.'

'No Mairig. Mother: not me.' And the paintings from the church alcove crowded into my mind: the devils gathered round the naked fleshy sinners and devouring them in black and reds and the angels on high with their luminescence and halos and I would forever be with the devils, I thought, "demoniac," and that boy took all of her ideas into his head and made himself sick from it and he was in the infirmary for days and the nice mairigs in the infirmary said it was bruised ribs and something else; and the boys whispered it was because I was not clever enough: stupid Vahé, you pay and pay with your flesh and the Mairig will cut off our hands and our feet and lame we will enter the gates of Heaven, she says; and better to be beaten and lamed than to suffer eternal damnation and if only I were cleverer, I think, it is because I am not enough until I see that wretched boy at our gates and know that He has answered what I asked for (and so eventually the wife, the children, a house, nice shoes) and his flesh for mine own. Yes. Vostanig saved the Turk-dog.

XXVII

BECAUSE KNOWING IS FLEETING, like memory. Something known emerges and *is known* thought and perhaps I say it; thinking *it is because we are animals*. And however we think it or tell ourselves different: we are flesh bone heart livers and tender-footed in the early days of summer and hungry and cold and sad and caged-sad and the cage-makers also (bone heart and livers). We eat and fuck and conquer that parcel of land that some animal has lived on for more than two thousand years: does the millenary living make it his? (If I have never lived there is it not mine? Is Kharphert in old Turkey no more than a daydream, a vision, a notplace? And if I can never be from this place, because in the Lebanon blood never changes to water, and you cannot change your clan, confession, your race—then from where?) Or is the bone heart livers and tender-footed in the early days of summer and hungry and cold and sad and caged-sad now become a cage-maker (cabinet-maker paperhorse-maker maker of long walks)? Because if we are they then Jumba is Vahé and to look at him and know it is to be filled with shame and loathing—at his cagedness and for Ali and the keeper and the darkskinned gardener and Juliana and Monsieur Gembali and the rich ladies in Hamra shopping the Italian shoes and matching handbags and the fat merchants and Vosto and Andranik, Mairig, Béatrice (I love her). Because to see Jumba is to see: savage violent beastly and he is correctly caged for our viewing pleasure. See him *he is happy*. But when I know for that fleeting moment, the knowing surges forth *it is because we are animals* and if I do not act it will go away, do not write it down, it will vanish into ether like memory and false sentiment. And then I will not act on it, I will not kill that monkey on a Sunday in May while he is smoking his cigarette and looks up at the steel bars cutting the sky. I haven't brought a fishing knife with me and I don't slam it through his eye when he reaches out for his cigarette, the blood skipping out of the eye and down the knife to my hand: in this one moment, the first and last, we look into each other's eyes and I see him in all of his animal barbaric fucking heart and liver and mouth and dark-eyed gloriousness: the most beautiful being I have ever beheld—I see that all of the beauty in this earth is in his eyes and the look of sweet relief on his face; he is freed from his cage and I love him, I have always loved him. And I have done something beautiful, made by slaughter and freeing because he doesn't want heaven to get his mother back or Urakayee or the old place they took him from when he was just a babe—the involuntary shudder, the small ape torn from his mother's teat and the place of his birth and no-walled paradise: he wants a free spirit and I give it to him, cut it for him, and I shall do it for me also. Pull the knife out of his eye against the cartilage and flesh and he falls forward against the bars and notmoves and I turn the knife back and aim it at mine own eyes, to take the mendacious sight and to release with my thrust my spirit: knowing I'll never get her back or any of it or know it better than I do. And I am doing it, the knife descends and my hand is steady and I see the steel attenuated point of the knife red silver and then nothing. I cannot see. And the knowing moment is gone, vanished like tobacco smoke, and I am on my back, open my eyes, smoking, and it is the late afternoon. What was I thinking? Thinking: *tomorrow I'll get up. Get up and go to the zoologique and feed the elephant some peanuts.*

XXVIII

I DID NOT DO IT OUT OF LOVE, or a premeditated lust, but
rather, I think, out of a desperate convenience, a coincidence of
time and place and sentiment—you there willing, we standing
outside the restaurant and I tell you I've forgotten my billfold and
could we pass my flat on the way to the cinema? And we take a
taxi to the corner of Rue Azhar and Rue Madhat, next to my old
flat where I'd lived for nine years and there is an old lady dressed
in head-to-toe black sitting on a small stool outside the building
and we don't have a doorman in this building and I ask you if
you'll come up for a moment while I retrieve my billfold and you
say it's not a problem and then it's the usual man heaving onto
the woman. And we marry because: you came with me to my flat;
I invited you and you accepted; it was convenient and not un-
pleasant to do so. And you carried a small darkness beneath your
eyes which I thought I could love and I told you Oui, je t'aime.
But I have wondered over these many years what made me do it
at that particular moment: prevaricate in front of the restaurant

as we stood there waiting for a taxi; why the fib about the left-behind billfold? I knew, as well as I knew anything, what it would mean for us to be physically intimate and you were not the first goodgirl Armenian girl I had dated, but I never questioned my act or the lie itself, it simply came upon me: we are standing outside of Uncle Sam's, the southwesterlies have picked up and it is getting cooler, and you are telling me again how you love films with the American actor Cary Grant and then, notthinking, I say it: *I've left my billfold, would you mind a small detour?* And you of course have never been to my flat, and rarely to this part of town, and I can see you are nervous, you twist your hands together in the taxi, your knees are pressed together tightly and I am interested and beguiled by your nervousness, your nervous scent, and I am overcome by a desire to fuck you, at that moment, at any cost: even the cost of marriage. But I don't think of marriage then, I think of your sex and how it will look and smell and putting my fingers there and my mouth and all of this while we are driving across town and the horns are blaring the southwesterlies pick up and I'm about to make you my wife without planning or foresight but out of a desperate coincidence, this convenience of time place and sentiment—we are standing outside of Uncle Sam's and I get a hard-on and say this thing about my left-behind billfold (the hard-on first, then the unplanned speaking), then your nervousness in the taxi and my desire to see your cunt, and then the usual man heaving onto the woman.

But I don't regret, I never do, I remember that moment with a kind of tenderness; tenderness for the man I was then and the woman that you were, and all that was possible between us: the unborn children; the larger flat in Ras Beirut; nice things. And I am curious how it came to pass, almost on a whim: if only you'd said No darling, or if we'd traveled downtown instead of south, or if I'd not become aroused at the precise moment we stood in front of Uncle Sam's anticipating the ride to the cinema, then perhaps I'd hardly remember you now, or your scent, your smooth back, wouldn't know the geography of your body and not have become accustomed to it, nor betrayed it later, much later, with the girl in our conjugal flat.

XXIX

BECAUSE WHEN I SAW HIM I became clever and in our Nest
only the strong clever boys succeeded. Because I forgot it and
then later remembered: that all of us orphan boys were liars. We
lied about what we'd done, where we'd been, whom we loved;
the pain in our foot from a sharp piece of tin; a stomachache;
drinking the wine in the rectory; and we deceived our friends and
lovers and the mairigs and Mairig and Hayrig and anyone else
who could forward our success or by a word, blow, adjudicate
our demise. I saw him arrive, I was on my way to the office to de-
liver a message about one of the boys and it was quiet in the yard
and it was a cool spring morning, the westerlies came in off of
the water and the sky was big above me—except that I added the
cool and westerlies and sky later; what I remember is less precise:
a wretched ugly boy standing outside our gates and he is quiet
just stands there and sees me looks at me, says nothing, looks as if
he's been standing there all night: his clothes are wet and the bit
of hair on his head matted and I can see he is afraid because he

looks it. So I approach this boy without now remembering the cool breezes the sky above us: just this picture of him in grays transmuted by my mind: I walk toward him and he unmoves, stands, and I'm sure I say hello and ask his name (but I also do not recall the words I used): what then? this: that he would save me. That I would be saved and that now I could succeed, now I would not have to kill myself, now I could be stronger and more clever than this neonate. And later when I slapped him and I fucked him I was happy and for this I have no remorse or sadness: because all that we could do in that place was to survive and to survive one had to be strong and clever and I learned that I could do it and it did not haunt me or plague me in any way: I became a happy boy and a successful man. And know that I am a liar, know this: when Jumba died (and Vosto died and Béatrice, yes, she has gone, and Juliana you also) I felt sadness well up in me and behind this well-up I remembered and re-remembered a few things about my childhood, and I have not tried to be honest because honesty is itself a false modesty and the lie is truer because we live by lies and propagate them as easily and readily as one propagates the memory of an unjust slight or the myth that we returned the slight with blows and later will swear it is true, and perhaps all of the lies together will form some kind of truth about the man, the orphan, the refugee—a circling of lies to hollow out the truth of this life and perhaps its only conclusion is its hollow-ness emptiness: the ragged round left by absence of affection and knowing and perhaps this man can only know peace through the big sky and blue wide band and chained smoking beast who him-self can only know peace when he smokes his cigarette and lies on his back, the world dissected by the protean steel bars. To lie is honest. My lies are my history and they have altered with time, they have changed as my memories have changed because more than fourteen years ago, before I was married even, I looked up and saw Vostanig shining my shoes on Hamra and we reminisced about the Nest, but I at first did not recognize him and he recognized me and we chatted about the horrid Mairig and her cane and our hahaha when the wine was taken from the rectory flask and you see I didn't remember him then (a lie): I remembered the times we had been allowed to swim in the sea, the boy Aram who'd died of appendicitis one winter morning, the Bible readings and the stupid boy who was beaten because he fell asleep right in front of the Mairig, and I told him so and I could see his face fall when I told him (lying) I don't remember you, no not at all, and I lied to myself about it afterward for enough years that it became the truth: I never saw him on Hamra, I didn't know him, that was not me—some other Vahé, some horrible vile Vahé who lived in an orphanage and was beaten there and fucked there and suffered abomination and: not me. Not me not me not. I didn't know him and I told myself I did not and it was true, I made myself in to someone else, another Vahé Tcheubjian: a man who was birthed in September, a man who married a goodgirl Armenian girl, and all of it was new and true until Vosto's very own specter began to haunt me (began it on my birthday last year: 26 September 1963) and I couldn't be sure if my lies had created the djinn or the boy himself not forgiving the unjust slight, remembered after death, would have his vengeance upon me: a re- and re-remembering of my life. Now I have no assurance as to what happened or did not and it matters little. What matters? The sea of course. The sky and the blue of the Mediterranean, which has always comforted this animal as nothing else ever could. I am sure the Lebanon tried to save me with her geography the mountains and cypress and twice-bloomed jasmine and wisteria and red brick roofs and the sweets the delicacies which make the mouth water—with all of her bodied earth and perhaps she did and perhaps I have not died in the sea after a long swim, Juliana at the shore yelling at me to not do it; and the sealight as always is the most beautiful. And if I were the believer it would be happy and finis: the sad lost boy, the unhistoried boy, re- and re-remembered: made good.

XXX

BECAUSE, it was like this:

—— Monsieur, you like your shoes shine?

—How much?

—Twenty-five piastres.

—Go ahead.

—You like them shiny?

—Yes.

—(*in the dead tongue*) You remember the Nest, sir?

—It's hot today.

—Yes, monsieur.

—Hotter than yesterday.

—Yes.

—Here, take it.

—Thank you. Until next time.

—Goodbye.

XXXI

AND THEN at ten eleven discovers that he cannot do it any longer, that he will not, that the good listens first place and handsome football runners, the listens and yesyesyes boys cannot be him, will not be, and knows that His plan, the rod, the avatar will speak and speak, they want more and more and so he won't do it any longer and learns, as he has learned his numbers, the dead tongue, learns not to do it: to notlisten the Mairig, the Big Garo, Bedros, the Mr Hovannes because that other Vahé says: I would kill her if I could do it—sneaked into her room and steal the sweeties she keeps and take a knife from the kitchen and hide it in my trousers until it is too late in the night and then sneak out of the bunkhouse and into the courtyard and across it and the half-moon illuminates my path across the courtyard and open the gate to her house and in the night the creak and spit of cold metal open it slow and see the shrubbery the three orchard trees the tile bench they'd made for her the path they'd made and carried the rocks for and laid it for her and all the plantings and shovels and heaves they'd done it because (they didn't choose to) to honor the Mairig who cares for us, they'd written it in a book and the book sent with the photographs of the cleaned-up pressed (happy) boys to America and they'd sat up straight as instructed and donned the new photograph clothes as instructed and situp-straight, straighter (like a rod, she says), and the rod descends and for the first time in two years she beats him on his head and back and shoulders and he thinks: I am no boy to be beaten I cannot do it any longer and sits up straight and she moving through the ranks of boys swinging it down and then moves to the front row of 'her boys' she calls them and the photograph taken and sent off to America because never seen and afterward he will notlisten, walks to the gate, opens it opens her front door (sees the furniture the rugs the boys' hands have made; the bowl of fruit) and opens her bedroom door and finds her there, she is sleeping and she is naked sleeping and he climbs on top of her (*like a monkey* he thinks) and pulls the blanket from her and holds the knife to her throat and cuts her fucks her bites her teat and sucks it and she is awake and notspeaks and he uses his fingers like a cock and he uses his knife and he fucks it and she smiles because she wants more of it, more of his red and wanting monkeyprick, and he does it, gives it to her, loves her kills her for good. She says　　　　　——because at ten eleven he will not listen, he notlistens now, and waits he bides his time until sixteen when he can leave this place and he can have his own place (his own bed, his earnings)——he waits now, patient even, for the seasons to turn and turn him to the fall nineteen thirty-three when he will leave this place and he will not return, he swears to himself that he will not turn his head to look back and say goodbye and until sixteen, thinks, I'll notlisten to her to the other boys to the Mr Hovannes and the other teachers, I'll wait wait until I can do it and then I will, I will walk out of the front gates and never return, or ever spare a thought or a glance for this place, I won't even look northward after I leave: I'll stay in the center of the city and keep my back to the north, never give it a hello or yesyesyes or a nod: not ever again. And I will, I'll take it out of me, unremember it for all time.

XXXII

IN SOOTH, on some days I would like to find the person responsible for this: this life, this man that I am and the life that I have subsequently lived and the life that I never lived because unable to—alone and not wretched always but yet always the wretch, the man made into something vile on some days, the man on his back, unmoving, the silent lost tongue, the absence of bones and her body to make it (the world) familiar: the man cast out; in exile.

(*do you see?*)

I cannot place blame on a man as one places a curse on him or seeks vengeance on him, but I would like to find him nevertheless: Enver Pasha, Talaat Pasha, Jemal Pasha—these Turkish pashas, rulers of an Ottoman Empire, their bodies unavailable, mythic: was it their flesh made mine (solitary, notlistens, *abandonné*)? Because: where is the man that took her from me? Who the man, that particular sentient breath named man who opened her legs who shoved her over a cliff into the river behind a stone building? Because just as the knowing is impossible, the man also is impossible, so it is not him I seek, but the system that makes him (such as me) into system-followers, men who follow the injunctions, believers, the rules and customs, say: Yes they are vile; Yes they must be intolerated; Yes here is the boundary of our village shove them out of it; Polluted; Unbeliever; Dogs; I didn't see anything, men; I was tilling the field, men; They are dogs, men; They are not men, men. Or perhaps it is not the he or the system man makes and man follows, but the why of it: are we so easily led, killed, defiled and humiliated and dominated and haunted then by our specters who cannot return either, who say to us notspeaking: you are no better than dogs unless you do it? And we do it: killers, defilers, shame, we lift the rod on high, we beat our children as we ourselves were beaten—we haunt the invisible passages of history: the unflowing river, the unlifted westerly, what you cannot see, say. *Because: the system is true. Because it is this way always. Because: civilized; necessary; kill the beast. On s'amuse, on profite.*

As a boy I believed that when I died all would be revealed: the killers, my parents and theirs also, and everything understood as if in a history book: Here darling, see us here, I am holding you as if in a photograph—here you are at birth, I give you a big kiss. Your father is delighted, a boy! Your grandfather carried you on his shoulder for days and singing all the while: la la la. This our village, your name, your brother. At this age I have seen in the sunlight and I have seen in the sealight that this place is all that I will ever see and that Mama doesn't wait for me in Paradise and no Baba no grandfather and no blood—because in death (I know) they will not be seeable for me, irreparably lost as I have lost God and Paradise to the sunlight sealight and long hot afternoons, smokes his Gauloises too much, and the sunlight is beautiful. The Lebanon and the Anti-Lebanon in the distance. The wonderful weather. I understand now, in this my middle years, that they gave us God in the orphanage like the rich will give a coin to the corner beggar—it's enough to keep us quiet and continually searching the horizon (not their eyes, don't see their new shoes and) and even anticipating death and loving it and always with this anticipation like a boy eagerly awaits the end of childhood and the *to come* more powerful than (their new shoes fancy automobile) the now of sitting on the street corner with my hand extended hopeful that one or two small coins would make this day of sitting fruitful. And there is no shame (in the extended hand) to their new shoes and fancy automobile and Paradise is just beyond sight, close your eyes to see it, and you there Mama and you also Baba. As a child, Mother, I looked forward to the dying and your form awaiting me at gates wide and heavy metal, I imagined your beautiful shoes and you also beautiful with soft, soothe, hands. As a boy I dreamed of it often and as a man I kept it in the back of my mind like one keeps stones in his pocket, blank and not looked at but heavy nonetheless, heavy soothing granite, the anchors for this boy of nothing. But I know now, and what has made me know?, I came to it slowly and of a sudden: looking up into the blue vast sky and out at the sea of a moment and over the years until now this my forty-sixth year I have realized, I have seen, what is before my eyes, what was there when we came down the mountain those many years ago: the blue band stretched wide, then the sea and white fish, then closer and the disappearing appearing waves until closer and then the floating tin and a girl's knickers. No gods in the sea, or in the blue heavens. It is this perhaps that made me sadder, but I think not Mother. Don't be sad for me. You must not be sad. You are, still and ever, for as long as the in and out of my breath, my own Mama: beautiful, gentle hands, you wrestle me out of myself and into the world—I made cabinets and long tables and high shelves for the ladies of Hamra and downtown and Ashrafiyeh. I have been a maker all of these many years, of cabinets and tables and smooth planks and long walks and a marriage and of love. In losing you and Heaven I can see the sea and the light the better; here I am as Adam, unchained from God and the new shoes that have forever scorned me; and freer: the man made back into an animal. I would like to stop (the in in out out) but I am not pressed. Quiet, slow, perhaps I'll make a small box and into it I'll place a letter to you and after I've made the box I'll write you this letter: Dear Mother, it begins, Bonjour!

XXXIII

—I remember when they gave it to you and we're all there
behind the mess house, my God that food they gave us those first
years, not food at all, the fatty soups and a meager portion of
black bread and how the strongest clever boys would make holes
in their wooden spoons so that when they served themselves
from the communal bowl they got more beans more fat? But my
God if the Mairig caught you, there was hell in the payment and
it was in that first year, first month even, a group of the big boys
had you behind the mess house and I couldn't see you, but they
were yelling at you and you probably didn't understand much of
what they said who can remember it now what they said and the
blows and later that night I remember you crying in the bunkhouse but not saying anything intelligible, not then because you
couldn't then, and they started calling you Vahé then, as a joke,
repercussed, see? And it was funny for all of us and we needed
to laugh have a bit of fun and it was not so terrible, was it? because it did make you back into one of us, the strong, the victor

pours pours pours: our own Vahé-boy—and you did slowly improve after that, become one of us, and after Vostanig that horrid
boy arrived you even had your own group to follow you, make
things for you, assist, and he then repercussed because the orbit is
well worn, footworn, and come back again but this time you the
perambulator on its path and he your very own monkeyboy carrying your bags your box and then you were victorious, weren't
you? hahaha—the strong one.

XXXIV

I went down to the lower hall of the orphanage one day and found a group of my teachers around a little boy. He was such a pitiful mite, covered with dirt and grime, his little head all broken out with sores, his tiny body covered with scabies. His thin, emaciated arms and shoulders were hung with a few filthy rags. He had just been picked up in the street. At this time the Kharphert orphanage, the Danish House, was overcrowded and our supplies were limited and we had been refusing to take any more children. After he had been cleaned up and fed I called him and one of the teachers to me and tried to find out who he was. When we asked him what his Christian name was he said only 'Mustafa.' We asked him his mother's name. He did not know, but did recognize the name 'mother' in his native Armenian. Although we named over all the native names of men it brought no response from him. Then we asked who his father was. He just looked at us in a dull, irresponsive way until finally, after a long time, a gleam came into his eyes and he replied, in Turkish: 'My father—why, my Heavenly Father.' And this was all we ever learned about that child. It was evident he had originally come from a Christian home but where that home was or who his parents were we never found out.

XXXV

ALTHOUGH I HADN'T PLANNED IT, I grew accustomed to
it: the rough edges of your feet; the untucked flesh, unrestrained
and marked skin; your body's odors and your body without
adornment; and I grew accustomed to the coffees and sweeties
you served me and all of the meals you made and tidy-up and the
laundered shirts, oui c'est vrai, and it is inexplicable to me then
how it happened, how over time (you covered up your darkness
and) you became more and more like the things you purchased,
something in the house and I was accustomed to it, to you and
your breath and your complaints, worries, but, and it is inexplicable, because as the years passed you and I living in this flat together, and eating together, we go to the zoologique, we have a
whiskey, we dance the circle dance at parties; we heft the image of
the couple at parties; and then, when?, it seems all of a sudden,
although I am certain it is not, all of a sudden, because I cannot
trace the precise moment of happened, but there it is—suddenly—
and it is as if I see you like some thing in the house, but all of it

through a veil of water and this water (seawater) refracts the light and it is all incorrect because you are next to me but it is as if you are one hundred kilometers and out of reach, and Juliana, over time, I became more than lonely in our marriage, as if the reminder of you, this refracted image that walked through the rooms of our flat and handed me kibbé and coffees made me more than lonely, more alone, not less, because this distortion reminded me of the distance between, and I became more lonely and then more, and then more than I had ever been (and then, yes, darling: Jumba, Vostanig's spectral return, Béatrice). And I am sorry that I couldn't find my way back to you; that our marriage became a container that held the lonely like a boy holds an empty soup cup and wants just a small amount, just the littlest bit more of some fatty soup. And I couldn't speak and speak it to you say: Juliana, your mind one place and mine another, because, darling, I had never learned this speaking, only the notlistens, the speaking Vahé was always some other boy, a liar, a boy who said the weather is nice today, yes I love the Ritas (to his workmates), the hahaha at dinner parties, and a tin of milk, a half kilo of rice, please: the Vahé you can see. And I have begun to understand that this thing which has long been in me, this beast, vogel, is of course my own flesh and blood despair and my inability to change what has come before (and to change what will come after), and me always the boy deposited upon the shore and running hell-bent with the other millenary boys for the unknown (sad inscrutable) Mediterranean. And if I left our flat to take the late-night walks along the Corniche and saw the drinking drunk men there, a few couples, and walking with my coat lapels held in one hand and the other hand lifts the cigarette to my mouth and away and smoking, walking, left you in our flat, alone (for years), to think who is this foreign and strange and sad man I married, who does not speak except for his request for coffee, dinners and to do this and that other thing?; but you should know it: I did and do love, but I can't feel it like other men do, and I'm sorry for that also: this notfeeling. But I'm sure it lives in me, like a kidney or like a lost photograph of a boy: he is an orphan boy from the time before; he is clothed in rags and his hands (if he has them) are hidden by too-long sleeves and his feet are bare and he has the look of the orphan, the look of sorrow and despair; and I never had it, only carried it inside, invisible, like that beast. Could you have seen it, darling? Could you have saved me, darling? To do it to do it, we are all of us alone and lost here, and I am sorry I couldn't have done it better than I did. And there is nothing for it but to tear it out of me, as you did Vosto, the beast must be defeated and its only defeat is death and if I weren't a coward and more the patriot I would do it now: run down to the water and swim in the sea, swim forever, forever held and—

XXXVI

THEY'LL TAKE YOU FROM ME. He'll come for you on a
Sunday afternoon and you'll take your small bag, your extra
dress and scarf and you'll board a bus with your father and you'll
head southward along the Beirut-Sidon highway until you reach
the city and then the camp and then the edge of the camp, your
family's one-room house and the festivities will begin the following week and everyone will celebrate and you will be beautiful in
a new dress and your coiffed hair and a piece of jewelry from
your fiancé who is too old for you, a farmer in his mid-forties,
and he'll see your sweet face and your sweet form and each night
he'll use your form like a man will sharpen his knives and fucking you and you cook for him clean everything mend the clothes
and bear child after child for this old man whose breath will stink
of tobacco and garlic and who, my darling, will no more understand your internal landscape than a farmer can know the banker's
league tables. And you'll not love him not hate him except perhaps if he has maltreated you and you will love your sons and

daughters and although you are exhausted I understand that it is a better life, the work work interminable, but in this case it is your family you serve—and you can kiss them, nuzzle their neck, lick their cheeks and love their feet and hands backs and thighs. You'll be a good mother, Béatrice. You'll love your flesh like you loved music and chocolates and when you remember Beirut it will be with a sense of relief that you are gone, and you will tell your children when they are older that the capital has its problems also, that there are thousands of Palestinians living there, that there are few jobs available to them there: the construction workers, domestics, fruit-pickers and shoeshine boys; and that a 'belt' has circled the city with its shantytowns and unwashed children and hungry desperate people and you will wash your own flesh and feed them (your husband a farmer): potatoes, parsley, bulgur, apricots and there are fig orchards near the camp and there are oranges to be eaten from the south on a special occasion, and the sun shines on this skin and you can see the ancient sea from where you live from where you live the girl Béatrice is happy. She can be at home here, remembers this place from when she was a child and she walked unadorned in the fig orchards and the apple trees and the almond blossoms and her mother kissed her and her sisters brother tickled her cheeks—and if her father is a stern man and if her husband is a quiet man, he works hard, then God has been good to her and at home she will darn sweaters, socks, trouser hems and she'll notremember her master from those Beirut years, she'll take him out of her, remember his girls, the yellow-red gloaming, a French song on the radio. And the foreigner, the Armenian, the woodworker man from two floors below her? His strange manner, his dark looks and he'd take her hand and say her name in his foreign-accented way, say strange, he a strange sad person, she thinks, *he wanted something and I unable to give it. Because: I became you Béatrice; I was the girl, the sad limps madonna girl for a girl who did not believe in madonna who owned no Christ who with a look undid this man and then redid him, like a ride on a tilt-a-wheel will make the world anew. You had no Virgin Mary? No man prostrate on a cross? For whom did you prostrate yourself, darling? Your Master Yusef, a good Christian, he made you a martyr to himself and I could have undone it, I wanted to (fuck you suck it from you make it) love the dark unspoken parts of yourself, I wanted to hear you speak Arabic in your funny way, your southern accented way, and we could have done it: overcome all of our invisible barriers, we could have done, made culture into a heap of dung, we could have made it done it loved ourselves the ancient sea the chimpanzee in the white-tiled box.*

XXXVII

BECAUSE PERHAPS the reason I couldn't find the words and
these many months since Vosto appeared I have been on this road
and walking, the perambulator, the Corniche walks, walking,
looking, seeking the words that could say it, could answer all of
the questions, could find the answer, the trick in the hand, a mys-
tery resolved. And each looking seeking takes me down a different path, a new byway, and all of it runs to nothing (to the sea)
because perhaps the reason the words were not right for the saying and I couldn't find the words is because the words themselves
cannot do it: cannot say it right. The merest beast knows it. The
stupid infernal wharf feline who brushes my leg on my walks
knows it; Jumba knew it also; that the sound of desire, of sadness, of joy, of rage—the sound of it, is the truest expression.
Jumba's pant-hoot high and sticky when the other chimp chased
him and he was throwing (hysterical) his shit at her and the pant-
hoot pitched hysterical—what could he have said (had he the vocal cords to do it) that would closer express than his pant-hoot

pitched in hysteria, his flying shit? And the wharf feline who brushes my leg, her miao expressing all of the desire for it: to be touched, please touch me, and all of the joy then in the drawn-down miao, the brushing and warble sounds her ecstasy. And man? What does he do? Bend his passion and joy and anger rage and sadness into abstract sullen word-sounds that take us away from the vrai sound, the thing itself. Just as when the man and woman fuck it, it is not the words that express in the fleshiest part of ourselves our fleshy desire, not the words, but the belly pitched moan, from the genital to the spine and seeps into the vocal cord: fuck me, it means, and we know it like we know how to breathe— and there is no space between the moan and the desire: it is the thing itself. And I think this is why I have always yearned for the moment of high-pitched desire, that falling away of words into the beast's pure expression—that: —its truth in this world of prevarication of obfuscation of language distanced lies. I want the body only and the sounds it makes—the truth of flesh; the boy suckling his mother, his   before he latches onto her teat (she hears it, recognizes his hunger pleasure). Armenian is dead. It was murdered in the summer 1915 when no word or sentence or lyric or ode to man's dignity or proclamation or newspaper article or pleading by the Patriarch or pleading by the girl before the soldier violated or letter or bill or identity card could say, say it so that it would be heard; so that the bodies could be pulled from the desert and put back into their homes; so that the men could be pulled from the ditches; the women and chil-dren and old ladies from the rivers; the babies from beneath the trees; the orphans from the orphanage and put back made back into who they had been—their tongue could not alter the smallest breeze; could not say them: nay. It could not say (for pity's sake, honor's sake) to the Turkish soldier gendarme kaimakam: *Please, sir. I am a man.* And hence it perished as perhaps all tongues are destined to—the truth, in sooth, can be found in unprevaricated unhindered unsymboled sound. The beast knows it, he is superior in this, but alas, he is stupid also *cannot make a gun* and dies for it, locked in his sooty steel cage; stares at the bars over his head—for forty-five years he lives in cagey squalor and dies and is thrown onto the garbage heap. None to miss him. To eulogize him. All of his kind filled the garbage heap years before his meat was deposited there. None to ever have imagined his suffering *I have imagined his suffering* seen his scary flesh and perhaps this the bind of it: or: the delicate recondite art of it: this not thing that pulls us from our bodies, makes us makers of things—that it can imagine us into places: I can daydream a boy, a chimpy, into being; I can release the beast his suffering.

XXXVIII

IF I INVENTED the wind and the rain, compiled them afterward to the you standing there outside our gates, then how do I know that you were there and not also invented by me and memory and the lies are indistinguishable from the truth: you were there in the wind and rain and rain-splattered and tired and hungry and sad: a sad lost boy from the time before. Did you exist Vostanig? And if I cannot be sure of your existence, then I cannot be sure of anything—of the many long walks along the Corniche, of Jumba and his Urakayee, of the Mairig and her long hot canes, of the blue around the bend of the mountain, mine own sadness, and this unspeakable beast inside of me, this unfeathered and unflying beast, which has been my unspeaking companion for as long as I can remember and now perhaps even it unexisted and maddened me. Perhaps I am nothing, a beastly corporal illusion someone thought up in the dark days of summer and pulled me out of the ether for his pleasure or pain, and relivened me and for what I would like to know? To what purpose? I would have liked to remain unexisted and ubiquitous like the sea out of view from my balcony window. I think it is true that I didn't want to exist and once existing wanted only the peace and the mountains and the warmth of her body, and I don't think I ever had it and I have longed for it all of these many years and now I would like only to unexist, not to die, but perhaps to kill that specter that imagined me out of the ether, that memoried me, has attempted to history the unhistoried boy, the unclanned boy, the orphan, refugee, and I would have liked only to remain so: unspoken because not speakable, because to speak me is to alter maim and transfigure the boy who wanted only to be loved: I can say it now: to have been loved and out and out and free. Unspecter me. I have always desired it. Out out and free: the sea the wind and the invisible force that brings us to the limits of our desire, to the edge of things, out. I have always longed for it.

XXXIX

BECAUSE I NEVER EXISTED. Because it was never me in the Nest with the hordes, the thousands of lost boys and girls. I wasn't the Armenian unnamed boy thrown onto a train in Eregli and unloaded by the Levantine coastline. I never lived in that place until I was sixteen years old and then told to leave and leaving living in the back of Gembali's shop until I was twenty-four and then letting a flat with some other boys, cooking rice over the single-flame stove. I did not hear the Arab boys speaking loudly on the street corner about the garlic-stinking talks funny Armenians: their laughter at my stiff accent and 'Where is he?' when I mean to say 'she.' I didn't work six days a week and ten hours each day and then the night school for two years to improve my Arabic and he and she. I didn't work and work and work for all of the years I can remember. And I didn't have my shoes shined by that Vostanig on Hamra in '49, months before he walked into oncoming traffic along the Corniche. And I didn't marry a girl at thirty-three and move into a larger apartment four years later in

Ras Beirut with the lifetime of accrued savings and then buy a new sofa and floor lamp. I didn't work and work and slowly buy more things until eventually a wireless and the futile attempt to have children and the work and save and work more. And I didn't have a glass of arak with Andranik last August. And I never saw Miss Taline walking down the street (her hands). And I didn't go to the zoologique on Sundays and smoke the Gauloises. And I didn't because I never existed, I didn't remember or forget any of it. And if you don't remember and if you don't recognize this flesh it is because it has all been in vain, the greatest fabrication: a lost dead boy retrieved from the dead time and dead places and in a dead tongue reviving and reiterating a life that was never lived, not seeded, out of place; impossible; irretrievable. Because I am no thicker than a skein of this smoke. Because this smoke is truer and plus vrai than all of this listless flesh. Because although I can feel the cracked tiles beneath my back and hear the long slow honk of the Fiat down in the boulevard and the lady upstairs beating her rug and the children and I know it is lunchtime because of the crashing gates and the garlic and butter smells, still I say: *it is not me*. I cannot speak. It is not me speaking. Some other Vahé speaks, one speaks and one notlistens.

Because here my mama loves me and I loved Béatrice and together we made it, freed the caged beast, his long lost days. And we can never get it back, return or unmake that which is completed and finished and then invisible: the blood attenuated across the decades into the next century and thinned and lost like the end of empires and the end of days, each day will end, as each life will cease, surcease, it is inevitable. And if we have existed we do not know it like we do not know our mother's name or bared breast as offering. And it is this, ultimately, that we all must know without knowing: that we are terribly alone, as separated by skin and blood and a thousand ideas as the specters are to the living and we will pass alone, the spirit unleashed in its terrible agony, ripped out by some invisible unstoppable resilient force that takes us from ourselves and makes us pass alone, whether or not we wish it, and whether or not we are prepared or clean or it is hot and the sun shines on this skin and unredeemed and not being, not existed, vanquished into the quiet, the hush, while the days continue, the nights are unabated dark. We unmade, undone by it all.

XL

YOU ARRIVED, it is a Wednesday in the spring of 1923; rains.
The boys have risen and completed their ablutions, the cold water, cold hands and one of the older boys cuts his foot on a sharp
piece of tin, it is a terrible cut and he cries and bleeds on the wash-
room floor and it is red all over and one of the older boys tells me
to go and get a mairig and I do it, leave the building and run
across the courtyard to get a mairig for the bleeding boy. The
older boy says, 'Kooskoos, get one.' I have gone and told her and
she hurries back to the boys' dormitory and I follow behind her,
more slowly, distracted by my desire to never return to that place,
a place where I am not happy and alone in my bed at night and
cold and the taunts and so wander over to the front gates (it is
quiet in the early morning air, it rains perhaps or has rained last
night and everything is wet concrete wet bricks wet roof, the sea
in the distance (I can't see it) is also fuller and I can hear the loud
crashing waves). I don't love anyone here. I have been here nine
months and I don't love anyone, my floor mat is a cold place and

I can speak but I don't choose to, and I can listen and understand, but to listen is to hear: Turk-dog, a shame to your race, the fucked-one and monkeyboy here and here, cheep cheep: open your mouth up; and I think this is not me, but some other boy, there is the monkeyboy, the Turk-dog, and then another one who lived in an old place and this boy walks across the courtyard and doesn't return to the dormitory immediately and it is cold and cold hands feet and his long white shirt is wet now from the rain and his legs are wet, bare, as are his feet and he makes his way to the front gate and then he sees him: sees a small and naked boy standing outside the gates of the Bird's Nest. He is a boy who has not eaten in many months and his arms hang down by his sides, his fingers are pressed together tightly as if he is waiting for me, waiting for the morning and the gates to open and admit him. I can see him. His hair is sparse and grows in patches, his body is covered in open sores. His ears loom large on a large head: all appears large on his head because his body is, by comparison, a bag of tied-up bones: his knees bigger than his legs, his arms hang at an awkward angle, you can count each rib, see each vertebra in his back. This is perhaps unnoticeable, who of us has not lived with the hungry beast? So it is not this that takes my notice, because on any given day there will be boys lined up and waiting and begging to be let inside, many are left by their mothers or aunties who cannot feed them, care for them and leave them here, but on this morning, it is only he and that thing which draws me to him, it is not him, he looks at his feet, notspeaks, even after I prod him with a stick through the bars of the gate, *What's your name? Where're you from?*, until I draw some blood from those tinny ribs, ribs that look like they've no blood to give up, but I would like an answer and of course Vostanig cannot give it. How did you get it? I would like to know, because what I see, what draws me to him, is the vogel locked inside his chest—there is a headless unflying unfeathered beast inside of him, presses against his skin, clavicle wings and the sternum make feet: where is the head of the beast? I scream at him, laughing, and he notspeaks and I prod him, bleed him, and then it comes to me: he will save me, it is this boy I've been waiting for and have prayed for and he'll do it, save the Turk-dog and then run away back to the dormitory, smiling, contented: the beast has come to save me. And although I understood then that with all things there is a payment to be made, and the orphan pays with his flesh and bone, what I didn't know, was unable to comprehend, is that the orphan can never repay his debts: it is a lifelong servitude, and it always unpayable, and it wants more and more—so that unflying unfeathered beast became mine and I could never get it out, not with all of the bodies of girls, the sweeties, the good wife, a flat on Rue Makdissi, walnut boxes and mahogany tables, new shined shoes—it is with me perpetually in this life like an inheritance, and pushes against flesh and unfreed and heavy, like the memory of those sad unorthodox childhood days when what we wanted was a little bit of bread and what we couldn't ask for because we didn't know it, like we hadn't known the sea until that turn round the bend of the mountain, the descent toward the blue band, was a little bit of tenderness. A round warm touch. Yes. Love.

XLI

IT IS THE SUMMER 1964. I am lying on my back and it comes back to me; harks back to that other summer 1915, the summer of our death and yet my birth two years later, mine own birth after the death of a race and our tongue—perpetually out of place now, exiled among the hortense, the twice-bloomed jasmine, red-tiled roofs and an inscrutable sad sea. How do I know something occurred if I myself have not been witness to it? How can the invisible history stories be so strong as to engender a hate that will lift a knife and plunge it into the flesh of another beast, a man; or to slaughter him with a rifle semi-automatic? I am no cleric; not a school man; I am no man to answer such questions, or even to posit them; I think: *what did I do to deserve this?*: why couldn't we have stayed in dark Africa? In the jungle and quiet and birds fly; and of dappled trees and each beast puts the babe at her breast and walking, swinging, through the jungle world. If Jumba had drawn me a picture, would it have been of my face? Of this beginning to wrinkle skin, and neck which droops and swags and hangs over the shirt collar; and the sideburns; the thick nose and brown eyes; the black shadows persistent dark beneath eyes; I slick my hair back from my head; I use pomade; my teeth have turned a yellowbrown from the tobacco and coffees and they are bottom-crooked and——; or would he have drawn the lines of his bars, the steel barriers? I am lying on my back and the car horns are blaring, there is a Fiat down below and I can hear its particular boom and rattle, and a woman beats a rug, her small prelingual child cries loudly, and Vosto asks me for a cigarette, please, he says, when we are fourteen years old; and Jumba is smoking also; and I would give Béatrice the tobacco but Rita has stolen my pack when she left today and all of the todays, the nows become jumbled, riff, they flow together as the tributaries will flow into the sea and become one strain of water indistinguishable from the other waters——because: all of it is me; all of it mine own images, mine own pictures (like the moving pictures); bold; brilliant; in colors, gray— what I think; see; dream up. The daydreaming boy would like a coffee. He would like a cup of tea. He would like a sweetie and he can hear the Fiat horn blares in the street, the street cleaner yells out that he will kill the truck driver and the truck driver's family and Juliana saying why do you have to do that? I can't stop it. I wish that the words could hold all of this: this thoughts; this hard urges; this sad and desperate boy who's become a sad desperate man. It is summer 1964, and it is hot today. Juliana has gone to stay with her brother in Johannesburg, 'To visit his children,' she says. She says, 'I'll return in September, when it is cooler.' Béatrice returned to Sidon and marries a farmer, a tin-collector. Jumba died in May. Rita has gone off to Broumana with her boys. Vostanig tells me (the specter): 'It's your own fault: a man who doesn't know how to do it right. Love right.' And very soon, I'll get up, gettup, and make a coffee and I'll eat again, cook something, and all of this will pass and Juliana will return (she will return! she will!) and Gembali will say, 'Welcome back from your vacances!'; and I'll make a walnut cabinet to commemorate my return, and a walnut box and put all of this away there; forever; for the eternal blackness that looms on each side of living, the before-living and the after—stretches out into infinity like the cosmos around the organ clamoring meat.

XLII

AND SHE DID, she was gone from one Sunday to the next, and the following Wednesday a new girl arrived from the south, she is ten years old and needs to be trained, Madame Yusef says, she is stupid yet. Béatrice is to be married to a tin-collector, Yusef says when I stop him in the lobby; her father came three days ago and they left together, they took the Beirut-Sidon highway south for thirty-five kilometers and the new girl is a cousin, he says, she also does not speak too much, eats candies like a monkey will eat nuts. These Palestinian peasants, he says, multiplying like dogs.

And I walked out of our flat and I left everything behind and I took a service from the Place des Martyrs, one headed south, it followed the Beirut-Sidon highway. And all the way to Sidon I stared out the window and the loud music played in Arabic and people talked loudly in Arabic and I could see the sea, the banana fields, the tomatoes and okra and the sellers at the roadside and the houses in the distant mountain villages and the Lebanon and the Anti-Lebanon in the distance. And I arrived in Sidon and be-

gan asking in the café: Béatrice Ghanem; Béatrice Ghanem lives
_____ and then turn right and then the place behind the bakery, a ramshackle place, the barman says, on the edge of the camp.
And I find the ramshackle place and there is a rooster walking in
the yard and some small (shoeless) children and a girl washes
clothes in a tub and it is getting dark and then darker and there is
no electric light and I go up to the door and there is no door and
I push the curtain aside and a woman sits in front of a hearth and
looks up at me and asks me in the guttural southern Arabic what
are you doing? And I say it loudly, so that she can hear: Béatrice,
انـا احـبك, and the girl comes out of the other room carrying a small
child and she smiles and she wears a white dress and we hug and
kiss and make plans and together we leave that place atop Raja
and it is good and clean and beautiful.

Because: I did fuck her on that Sunday morning two months
ago (loved her in the flesh). And perhaps she didn't want to (I
could not smell her arousal), but she a girl who doesn't have no
like the boy without a slotted spoon or another cup of that fatty
soup, and I tried to see her and see what she would like (the
chocolates a silk scarf once) but to not fuck it with Béatrice was
to be dead and I needed to live, needed her and her small prurient
form, the teat, the cunt, the backs of her thighs. I didn't beat her,
but I loved her and I tried to give her love; loved her cunt and the
smell of onion on my fingers and her sex smell mixed with it,
mixed in with the woods, the shaved pieces of walnut, oak. This
notlistens Vahé, he fucked her and loved her. *Oui, c'est vrai.*

I was sitting on the balcony swing and Juliana is making my
coffee just as I prefer it; she gives it to the girl, the girl brings it to
me. 'Sir,' she says, 'your café.' And I looked up at her then, at her

soft, soothe, hands, her prurient bosom, her green eyes the color of new leaves, and all of it returned in that moment, pushed forth, as if the beast itself pushed forth, forced this act, and I can't control its flight and I called out to Juliana from the balcony that I would like a gâteau from Michel's for Sunday dessert, that I must needs have it. Juliana's yesyesyes. The good wife, she gets dressed and comes onto the balcony and tells me she'll be home in half an hour; she looks tired and old today; she is fatter and old-looking, I think. I put the daily on the floor and I get up and I walk toward the kitchen and everything is tidy and clean in the flat. The girl is standing on a chair and reaching to the uppermost cabinets and putting something up or taking something down and turns and her Monsieur? I was the notlistens Vahé, the Vahé who must live— who must needs love her in the flesh. I am putting my hand on her calf and I am putting my hand on her thigh and my fingers are in her sex and (inutterable) does she cry out (in her southern gutturals)? (Bua bua bua.) She lies on the kitchen tiles. I have lifted her dress and torn her knickers; I am as aroused as I have ever been. I have had a hard-on for weeks; for weeks during the long days and nights since that afternoon in her master's salon (the cotton sheathed unadorned teat); I can't stop it. She is lying on the floor (Please please please), she is not hitting me; she doesn't slap me, scratch my face; cries: Bua bua bua. And let it be known: I was not the first, she was no virgin. Yusef had fucked my madonna girl and I cannot stop it, I can't hear the girl's cries, don't hear them until after the servant door in the kitchen opens and Juliana is standing there with a pink tied-up pâtisserie box and I must finish it, and Juliana sees me fucking the servant girl and the orgasm trammels through and only when I am finished do I hear the Bua

bua bua and then softly, hoarse, 'Please, sir,' in Armenian. Juliana has closed the door to the kitchen and I hear my girl, my bright child, her tiny words against the beast (in his tongue, the victor's tongue): Please. And it is that word, an awkward and poorly stressed 'please' that could not change anything (or save anything) but made this man, unequivocally and for all time, her triumphant swain; made me love her like I have loved no other, as I could not love my own wife of fourteen years—made her my very own Béatrice (because she'd had that other and vulgar Arabic name, Jamilah or Nabihah, before I gave her the good French)—my own blessing. The sooth flesh I required to get a little bit of it back, a small immeasurable ineffable return: inside that girl's flesh I was (say it!—Says): home.

XLIII

AND DOES THE WIFE return from South Africa when the summer vacances are finished, and tanned and thinner than when she left; a new coiffure; a stylish handbag she is holding at the airport; a new crepe de chine dress? She returns in September, and after she disembarks from the aeroplane I kiss her on each cheek and I am holding a cigarette in one hand and kissing her cheek and she remarks how thin I've become, 'You look like a bedouin,' she says, and I take her carry-on luggage from her hand. We are in a taxi leaving the airport and she tells me how her mother will stay on with her brother for another month to visit with the children, and how his girls are beautiful and refined and the boy is tall and delighted with collecting large insects and loves the cinema. She talks long in the taxi, looks out of the window and remarks how it is all the same since her leaving in July, tsks when we pass the tin shanties and haphazard shacks by the roadside, where seventeen years earlier the United Nations had handed out the white tents when the refugees first arrived from Palestine.

And she doesn't mention her affaire de coeur with Dickran, her brother's best friend in Johannesburg; this man who made her happy and then unhappy in the space of two months; a man who longs to return to Lebanon; who hates the dirty dark African, the white Africans who think he's dirty, dark; who has tired of the black whores and was happy with his friend's sister and their secret furtive encounters (the first time in the storage room of the shop he manages). And so Juliana has returned, thinks she can bear it now, now that she has had her own sordid (storage room gropings) affair, and that it will take the image of her husband fucking the servant girl, the dark shameful illicit thought pictures, from her mind.

And they'll resume their lives he thinks, she returns and he has risen, bathed, made himself a cup of coffee, he would like another cup of coffee when they arrive home, and she'll do it for him: make his coffees, launder his shirts, whiten the floors, cook the meals, make the shopping lists for more chicken more rice another half kilo of legumes. She'll be the good wife and he will do it, be the good husband, works and works and entertain the friends and lunch occasionally at the Saint Georges; perhaps they'll eat garlic chicken at a roadside restaurant with pommes frites and a green salad; and next summer they'll rent a flat in the mountains, in Aley, and he'll buy the daily from a shop in town, from the shops he can see the city of Beirut down below and below the city the vast blue belt of the sea; and they'll travel abroad the year after that and visit Juliana's cousin in Lyon and they'll do it, he thinks, they'll do it they'll do it, for as long as the days, the hours, continue apace. *I have a wife* thinks *and she has returned.*

XLIV

IT IS A SUMMER of jasmine 1986. They will arrive at his apartment in the late afternoon and the sun is still a two fingerband above the horizon, he can see it from where he sits and he says to them that it is hot today; the smell of jasmine fills the evening air. He rarely leaves the flat and when he leaves it is for the half kilo of rice and a tin of sweet milk if the grocer's boy has it. It is also a summer of war and there have been many such summers (eleven) already. The grocer's boy (he still thinks of him as a boy even though the boy is now a man and the father of three children) runs the shop across the street and on days when it is quiet and cease-fire he lifts up the metal shutters and sells the vegetables and tins he's been able to accumulate (the jasmine blooms on all of the summer days unceasingly and unwatered either). The bullet holes mortar shells in the sides of the buildings make a regular pattern and each building is like a young girl from the time before: of ribboned plaits and knee-length dresses and ruffles and all designed with the polka-dot fabric of their dresses like the outsides of the buildings now and this pattern returns time to the sidewalk gardens, the low-sloping red-tiled roofs, a rooster crowing, the clean and white everywhere and the cleaning truck passes by each morning and the ladies getting their hair coiffed and a girl with her long plait (unribboned even then) is biting her nail and her gait is uneven, her calves tight and beautiful against the polka-dotted dress she wears; there are flowers in the flower boxes and long days and piles of mutton and so many small dishes filled up for the mezzé (no: cracked open sidewalks, the potholes, the burned-out Mercedes hulls in front of the shop, small and large red handprints on the walls, the gray-dirt exterior of the buildings, stained, the dark gray diesel air, the piles of garbage, the shut-up windows and metal shutters shut-up. No front line (the Green-line) cuts the downtown, there is no longer a downtown, no Cinema Rivoli, no queue of services waiting, their horns loud in this city, pass in front of the Banque Suisse, there is not a Banque Suisse, no bordello behind it, nothing drives south to Sidon, no transport east or west; they have made the place a graveyard, a green weed mottled notplace; made the one city into 'East' and 'West' (and Christian and Muslim); made confessions into territories.) See the gardenias grow in Madame Renard's garden, see the flowering acacia in May, the swept-up streets and the street cleaner who wets the street daily to clean it and keep the dust down, the families out for a stroll with their boys Justin and Georges sucking greedily on a sweet-ice, Rita is having her hair coiffed in the new salon, the girl Béatrice is tucking her socks, Juliana will be home later, and the sea: all of the flora in bloom and the time before the eleven summers is the city's Season. La dolce vita. When we could have been better, when the refugee was relieved, when the sun was setting and hot and the girls plaiting and the women coiffing their hair; the sea not filled to by a five-story garbage heap. The eleven years of garbage do not reach out like an outlet with the loads of Coca-Cola bottles and plastic shopping bags and the shit and the tins of sweet milk and sunflower oil bottles and olive oil bottles and the rest of it, human detritus, uncollected for the eleven years and piled up higher than a five-story edifice so that he can see the sea but he must now look over the new tower. When the boys come to his apartment—"Tcheubjian," the boy is wearing a red handkerchief tied around his head, he switches the rifle to the other shoulder. The old man doesn't rise from the armchair where he sits; he sits facing the sea, the doors are open to the balcony and the seaview. (And Juliana has gone to stay with her mother in Ashrafiyeh in East Beirut—has begged him to leave West Beirut; 'WestBeirut?' he says, 'we live in Ras Beirut: 55 Rue Makdissi, 4c B; we have lived here all of these many years and I'll not go, not leave this place; my home.') So the four approach the old man and one closes the door (it has been left unlocked) and the boy wearing the red handkerchief switches the rifle back to his right shoulder and pulls a pistol out of his jeans pocket. 'When the boys come to his apartment, la la.' (Not, and not in the dead language: We told you to leave, that you must move to the other side; that there are two cities now—this one for us, the other for you. We told you to go. We told you and you notlistened. *And in the eastern neighborhoods of this city* thinks *this same conversation, different boys.*)

The speaking one says: And you will never get her back, not for all of your crying or sucking on shirttails.

The boys are laughing (really they are as tall as men, he

thinks); he thinks he hears them hahaha. The one with the pistol (is he not the grocer's boy?) approaches and places his gun against the old man's neck and what man makes and what man unmakes then. The five-story heap of detritus, the M-16 rifle on the boy's right shoulder, this building old now and polka-dot dress, Vosto, identity cards, calendars, curtains, Gauloises all of them, the foreign books, a Green-line, the yesyesyes, the moving pictures, the sweeties, the zoological gardens, a small wooden box, the bent-down girl tucking her sock her plait unribboned, steel, my sad and lonely Vosto, confessions, history, and   Not the sea not the weather

(and he would get up from the chair and he would walk out the balcony doors and lie on the cracked white tiles because it is cooler on the tiles, they preserve some of that morning's cool, and thinks: *I am laughing also and I am comforted. It is hot today. And tomorrow? Tomorrow the sea the weather, beautiful and free.*)

ABOUT THE AUTHOR

Micheline Aharonian Marcom is the author of the novel *Three Apples Fell from Heaven*. She lives in Northern California.